Kuriously Krazy

T.C. McFarland

Copyright © 2024 T.C. McFarland

ISBN: 979-8-218-37088-6

Published by All Challenges Mastered, Inc.

Edited by Jacqueline Harris

Cover illustration by Kiara Stebbins

DEDICATION

The Dark Side of Trauma

This book is dedicated to Karen Lime and everyone that suffers from traumas that can lead to mental illnesses. Trauma is a haunting force that can leave deep scars on our souls, leading to the development of mental illnesses and disorders. Trauma can stem from childhood abuse, devastating accidents, or shocking loss, which can create a breeding ground for mental illness.

One of the most disheartening aspects of trauma is the ripple effect it has on our world. It's like a pebble thrown into a serene pond, causing waves that reach far beyond the initial impact. Trauma tends to infiltrate every aspect of our lives, eroding our relationships, self-esteem, and overall well-being. By shedding light on this darkness, we can come together to support and uplift those who are suffering.

Together, we can create a safe space where others feel comfortable seeking help without judgment. Let's educate ourselves, spread compassion, and advocate for mental health support.

ACKNOWLEDGMENTS

With a pen in my hand, and words in my heart, the JJK Crew supported me while I poured out my soul with this creative art. To them, I owe a great debt, for their support and dedication that I will never forget. They have stood by my side through thick and thin, supporting my journey when it first began.

Again, this would not be possible without GOD placing gifted people in my path~ Another Masterpiece! To JJK Crew (Jackie, Jamel, and Kiara), my pillars and rocks, they are my inspiration, my strength, and my external flames. Much gratitude!

To my hearts and my heartbeats! The support and encouragement is overwhelming and I love you all SO MUCH~

In loving memory

My Mother, Gladys C. Dixon

My Father, Thomas Dixon

My Brother, Marvin L. Dixon

And to all of my ancestors who became

Angels to watch over me and my family.

~

Sincere gratitude to every reader who purchased this book.

Thank you for helping me support my community efforts.

Chapter I: The Delicate Confrontation

The Face to Face Encounter

I can't BELIEVE that Bitch drove away. Karen utters as she stood there in disbelief watching Charlice drive off in a black Mercedes. All she was trying to do was ask that high yellow heifer a question about William.

As she paces back and forth, she is slowly hitting her left thigh with her left fist. She glares at Charlice, the high yellow heifer who has just driven away, and says, using her most professional tone, "All I want to know is what business do you have with my husband? I know that you are in the real estate business. Are you trying to find him a new place to live? Are you selling him a house? What is your business with my husband? I am his wife. I have the right to know."

Karen stops pacing and clutches her hands together in excitement. She gasps, "Ahh! Is he surprising me with a new house? Oh, that must be it because you know he and I are getting back together. We just needed some time apart, but we are going to put our family back together. I just love that man."

"Oh, what did you say?" Karen pauses and leans over looking at the empty parking space where Charlice had been parked. She was trying to make sure she heard what Charlice said.

"Oh! You are happy for us." Clutching her pearls in modesty, "Thank you so much."

Shamefully looking down at the ground, Karen whispers, "I must admit. I have made some mistakes and I haven't been the perfect wife." Looking up at Charlice stoned face, "But Will and I were made for each other."

Karen looks in Charlice's imaginary eyes with clenched teeth and no smile and proclaims, "No ONE can come between us. Like our vows say, 'Til Death Do Us Part." With the last word, Karen struts off and heads towards her Range Rover.

Before Karen could finish her dramatic exit, Sam, a stylist in the beauty shop that Karen just left, comes from what seemed like nowhere. Looking around confused, Sam asks, "Umm Kur'n. Who the hell are you talking to?"

A little startled Karen swings back around thinking Charlice was about to clap back at her but she only sees Sam standing there with his arms open and his wrists bent backwards looking perplexed. Karen burst out laughing. "Sam, you startled me."

Sam, still looking around for another person, says, "Well you confused the hell out of me. I was locking up the shop and I heard you going in on somebody. You were having a deep conversation. So I came over to listen. Cause girl you know I'm nosey. Then I got even more befuddled when I sauntered over and didn't see a damn thing except you. What's going on? That fine ass husband of yours got you seeing spirits or something?"

Karen tapped Sam on his shoulder in laughter. "No Sam. You're so crazy. You saw that woman. That Charlice, Lou's best friend. She was just there. You didn't see her?"

"Ummm NO!" Sam answers.

"She must have driven off when I turned to leave." Karen looks around.

Sam gazes around and rolls his eyes. "I only saw you, Kur'n."

"I was asking Miss Thing about her dealings with my husband and she was being vague. So I was questioning her. Like that's my man and you need to tell me what's going on. I figured it out though. I still don't appreciate her being so dismissive concerning my husband." Karen folds her arms and rolls her eyes.

Sam stares at Karen. "What did she say? She's probably screwing him. That's why she was probably being vague. Hell, I would screw him too. Kur'n, your husband is fayinne. How could any woman or man resist that? Umph!" Sam shivers just thinking about William Lime.

9

"Oh no!" Karen interrupts. "It is not like that. William is buying us a new house. We are getting back together. You know. He loves me. William wants us to have a fresh start in a new home." She smiles enthusiastically like a little girl going to get some ice cream.

"Oh good for y'all." Said Sam, sarcastically, as he quickly sashays to his car. *That bitch is as crazy as a bed bug. If she only knew what I knew. I tried to give her a hint, but that went way over her head.* "I will see you next week Kur'n." Sam waves his arm out his car window as he drives off. "I can't wait to hear all about your new home."

"Okay Sam. Have a glorious weekend." Karen waves back just as happy as a lark. Then hops in her Range Rover, does a quick lipstick check in the rearview mirror and drives away.

Sam immediately grabs his phone and calls Sandy.

Sandy answers with a chipper tone, "Hey Sam! What's up?"

"Sandy…I am so-so-so-so sorry." Sam says, sounding remorseful.

"Sam, what is it?" Sandy sounding concerned. She sits down waiting for Sam to break the bad news to her. *Who died?* She thinks to herself.

"Sandy!" Sam breaks down pretending to sob.

"Sam, what? Take your time." Sandy asks, getting a little

10

anxious.

Sam yells, "SANDY! That bitch Kur'n Lime is cray-cray."

Sandy burst out laughing. "Maannn, you had me concerned. I thought something was really wrong with you." She pauses to catch her breath. "I told you. Nobody wanted to believe me. What did Crazy Karen do now?"

Sam proceeds to tell his story. "Chile I was locking up the shop minding my own business. Then I heard people arguing. You know my nosey ass. I headed in the direction of the conflict. You know just in case someone needed a witness or something. And so, I could make out what was being said."

Sandy laughs because she could visually imagine Sam's face as he was headed towards the noise.

Sam continues. "I walked around that Range Rover and low and behold it's that crazy ass Karen standing beside her vehicle just hitting her thigh and talking. Just going on and on about how she ain't perfect. William and her are getting back together. She loves him and he loves her. Blah! Blah! Blah!"

Sandy laughing asks, "Who was she talking to?"

"NO ONE!" Sam busts out laughing. "Not a MF'n soul. I was so confused. So, I waited for her to take a breath. Then I interrupted. And asked her who she was talking to."

"Who did she say?" Sandy asks curiously.

"She said Lou's little friend, Charlice."

"Charlice? Does she even know Charlice?" Sandy probes sounding confused.

"Well," Sam laughs. "She will now, Honey. According to Lou, Charlice is William's realtor and new side piece; but you ain't heard that from me. Charlice has been helping William find a new house for himself WITHOUT Kar'n."

"Oh my! Without Karen? That is going to send her crazy ass WAY over the edge. According to you, she may already be there. But… she does talk to herself when she gets stressed."

"Oh yeah! You did tell us that she talks to herself. Ain't nobody believe you but we should have with as much time as she spent BONDING with you." Sam laughs.

"Bonding?" Sandy inquires. "Oh, you got jokes? She was not trying to bond with me. She was taking up my time because she don't have any friends. I think I was way too nice to her."

"Girl, I know. She spent more time in the shop than me. You spent a lot of time with her. She just would NOT leave your chair. Oh my God! And the way she stayed in the mirror. That was crazy. Why would she think it was okay to stay in your chair all day while you were trying to service other clients?" Sam shakes his head.

"She is crazy. Nobody would believe me. Because she

12

would stay in my chair all day, I would end up having to stay late with my other clients. She would go off and talk to herself. She would be laughing to herself. Fixing her makeup in the mirror. Half the time I couldn't tell if she was on the phone with William or planning one of her fancy socialite events or just talking to herself. You see why I took a leave of absence from the shop? I had to get my mind right. She was just too much."

"I really didn't understand the situation. I mean why didn't you ask her to leave or just tell her to leave? Hell, I never would have let her interfere with me getting all of my coins." Sam asks.

"I did, many times. Lou even talked to her. Karen would say okay. She understood but then she would always find a way to hang out longer. Taking a leave of absence was the only way for me to get rid of her. Thank goodness Lou took her on as her client. She doesn't treat Lou like she did me".

"Because Lou ain't putting up with her bullshit." Sam laughs. "Lou would have just left her in the shop talking to herself." Sam chuckles. "What would she be talking about?" Sam asks.

"Everything and nothing. She would talk about her perfect marriage. Karen is delusional about William leaving her. She said he was stressed so he had to go live with his friend. I could hear him talking to her on the phone and I heard how he talked to her when he came into the shop. He was just tired of her. I am guessing that he wanted out, but

13

he stayed as long as he did because of the kids. He seems like a man who didn't want his kids to be raised in a broken home so he stayed longer than he should have.

Something must have happened that was his last straw with her, but I couldn't figure out what it was and she wouldn't talk about it. She would change the subject or go off and talk to herself about it." Sandy sniggers.

"William probably left her because he woke up and realized William Jr. is not his."

Sandy, cracking up, asks, "Why would you say that Sam? That is not nice."

"Sandy, as chocolate as William and Kar'n are, how the HELL did they get that white chocolate baby?"

"Sam, you are so wrong. That baby ain't that light."

"Humph! William Jr. is so light he could pass for Jorge Jr. or Jacque Jr. That baby is by a white man or something light, but that baby is not her husband's. William is a beautiful, sexy, dark chocolate specimen. Karen is the color of midnight. There is no way! When you mix black and black, you get BLACKETY BLACK!" Sam laughs at himself.

Sandy is cackling. "Sam, you are ignorant. I cannot with you."

"What?" Sam asks innocently. "You know I am right. What else she be talkin' 'bout?"

14

"Oh, her boring social events. You know her charity events, organizations and parties. She talks to me like I know these people. My clients just could not stand to hear her brag about what she had and her flawless marriage. It was too much."

"Oh goodness!" Sam thinks. "I'm going to have to go tell Lou to warn Charlice. Charlice needs to be careful. I have a feeling that once Kar'n has her mind set on something she is focused and vindictive."

"Yes. Yes, she is. When William left her and moved in with his friend… Umm what's his name?" Sandy asks.

"John." Sam stamps, knowing all too well of the situation and the man.

"Yes. When he moved in with John, she became obsessed with who was at his house. What time was William getting in? Where was he going? When was he coming home? What about the kids? What would their neighbors think or the parents at the children's school? What would her associates and socialites think? She was so concerned with what people would say? It was sad."

"And you had to endure all of Kar'n's drama." Sam shook his head. "You poor thing."

"Well now she is Lou's client. Lou's headache." Sandy pauses. "Poor Karen. I really do hope that she gets the help that she needs."

"My question is, does her fine ass husband realize how crazy she is? How did he stay so long unless he is crazy too?" Sam asked jokingly.

Sandy chuckles. "I don't think he is crazy. I just think he got so used to her behavior that it became normal to him. He was used to her shenanigans."

"I wonder, what was the straw that broke the camel's back? What made him pack up and go live with his gay friend?" Sam asks. "You don't have a clue? She didn't spill that tea? She didn't give any hints?"

"No! In her mind, they were still together. She acted like he was on vacation or something. I'm telling you Sam, she is delusional and any woman that gets mixed up with that situation had better be very careful."

"Understood. I hear you girlfriend. I will talk to Lou ASAP! So, I will see you tomorrow, right? You are working at the shop tomorrow? It's our Money-Making Day!" Sam screams.

Chuckling, Sandy replies, "Yes, I will be there in the afternoon. You have a wonderful evening Sam."

"You too Sandy. See you tomorrow." Sam blows her a kiss, hangs up the phone and immediately calls Lou.

Damn! No answer. He leaves her a voicemail message. "Hey Lou! You must be gettin' some. Girl, we need to talk. I got some hot tea for you so call me when you get a

16

chance. Smooches."

Sam continues on his slow trip through the busy streets of D.C. Thinking about William and Karen. William and Charlice. William and John. And just William. "Umph that man is fine. How did Kar'n even get a man that fine?" *I'm going to have to ask John that story. I'm not sure if John and I ever talked about that. John will tell me. I think he and I are good enough friends. After all, we do travel in the same gay circle. But I do need to speak to Lou. Even though she didn't say that Charlice and William are sleeping together, she did imply that it could happen. Charlice needs to be really careful. After what I saw today, we all need to be careful.* "Who knows what is going to make that woman snap or when she is going to snap? It's just a matter of time. Watch!"

***

Karen drives through the streets of D.C. replaying her confrontation with Charlice. Recalling Charlice's actions, Charlice's smugness and Charlice's overall arrogance. *I told her. Charlice?* "I think that's what they call her. I will ask Lou next week when I return to the shop to get my hair done. After all, that is Lou's best friend. I am sure she knows all the tea on her little friend. And she better tell me what I need to know!"

Who is this Charlice chic anyway? I don't like her attitude. It's always those high yellow girls who think they are prettier than everybody else. They think they can get any man they want. Breaking up happy families. Why was she so vague about her business with my husband? She must want him. She must be after him. After all, William is handsome. He's kind. He's a great dad. He's a great provider. He's great in bed despite his injury. I must admit he is a head turner. Who wouldn't want him? Um, let me call William and see what I can find out about this woman and their business relationship.

Karen proceeds to call William. "Siri, call hubby."

William answers sounding irritated, "Hey Karen. How may I help you?"

"Hello Dear. I know we just parted ways, but I think we should discuss the conversation that we had in the beauty shop earlier today."

"Oh?" William was puzzled. "Um…what do you want to discuss?"

"Well I just spoke to Charlene? Chartice? Charmaine? Char whatever her name is. She's such a nice young woman." Karen says sarcastically.

"Her name is Charlice Rice. She is a very nice woman." William corrected her defensively. "Where did you talk to Charlice?"

"Oh! I spoke to her in the parking lot of the salon. We had a nice chat about real estate."

"Okay?" William pauses. "What a minute…how did you

18

speak to Charlice in the parking lot, if you and I left at the same time?"

Karen is silent, getting her story together.

"Hello? Karen, are you still there." William queries.

"Yes Dear. I am still here. Oh! I had to go back to the shop. I thought I left my earring at Lou's station. But when I got to the parking lot of the shop, I found it between the passenger seat and the console. I can be so absentminded at times." Karen says hoping he believes her story. "Well anyway I saw her getting into her car."

"So, what did you two talk about?" William asks curiously.

"Well, I just asked her about finding a new house for us. I think we could use one. You know, for a fresh start. Wouldn't you agree, Dear?"

"WHAT?" William yells, shocked. "Why would you do that Karen?"

"Dear," Startled by William's response, she stutters, "I... I thought that's what you wanted. I thought...I thought she was looking for homes for us. For our family."

"Karen, when did I ever tell you that we were going to get back together?" William takes a breath to calm himself down. "Charlice is MY realtor. I asked her to find a home for me and the kids."

"Oh!" Karen pauses trying to process what William just

said to her. Giving a little awkward laugh. "Okay, but YOU said we were going to get back together. YOU said YOU wanted to work things out. YOU said you wanted our family back. YOU said…"

"Listen Karen." William cuts her off. "I am not sure what I want anymore. Of course I want my family to be together. But I need more time. You caused a lot of damage to our family Karen. Do you understand what you did? Do you understand what your selfish actions did to OUR FAMILY?"

"Will, I know that I spent a lot of money on material things which almost caused us to lose our home and almost ruin you financially. I understand that you lost trust in me for various things. But you love me and we are married." Quivering, she says, "After all the bible says, treat your wife with understanding as you live together. She may be weaker than you are. Treat her as you should so your prayers will not be hindered."

Karen starts to sob. At the same time, she waits for William's usual words of comfort and sympathy. *I know how to get him. He always falls for my tears.* In the past, she has been able to persuade William to compromise for the good of his family.

"Karen." William asserts, knowing that his estrange wife is some straight bullshit.

Sucking up her pretend tears. "Yes William?" She asks

20

softly in anticipation of his sympathetic words.

"Just stop! That is enough." William responds sternly as if reprimanding a mischievous child. "I have had enough of your manipulation. I can't take this right now. Yes, we discussed getting our family back together, but you have not changed and some things have changed for me. I need time to myself Karen, all by myself, alone Karen, without you."

"But William…" Karen renders, trying to get a word in.

"LOOK!" He yells. "I am working with Ms. Rice to find a new home for myself that includes space for the children. Ms. Rice is a nice young woman. Leave her alone Karen. I forbid you to contact her again."

Karen is dumbfounded and distressed, feeling like a wounded animal. She hangs up the phone. She can't believe he spoke to her like that. He rarely speaks to her like that. *He has never spoken to me like that while I am crying. Hum? He defended that Charlice woman. Why did he forbid me to contact her again? What's really going on? This sounds like an investigation.*

***

Karen arrives home. Races in the house; throws her Chanel bag down on the sofa. Then rushes down the hall to her office. She opens her laptop, logs in and does a Google Search for Charlice Rice. She finds a professional picture of Charlice. Charlice is sitting up straight as an arrow with a huge smile wearing a navy blue blazer. She finds another image of Charlice. She is standing in front of a house with a smiling family holding a sold sign.

"Humph! Chicago." Karen says out loud.

Karen switches to Google Images. A mugshot of a man pops up along with Charlice's same professional headshot from the real estate agency's page. Karen found several links to this same image. *The New York Times, The Washington Post, The Los Angeles Times, The Texas Tribune.* Karen clicks the *Chicago Tribune*'s link to the article.

"Uhhhh!" Karen gasps as she sees images of a light skinned woman whose face has been badly beaten. Her face is swollen and covered with black, red, purple bruises. Blood is exuding from the woman's mouth.

For a moment, Karen felt sorry for the woman. Then she reads the caption below the image. The caption read, Pictured: Images taken from the Chicago Police department case file. Victim Charlice Rice after being physical attacked and raped by her ex-boyfriend, former police detective Douglass Smith.

Karen smiles as she continues to read. According to the article, Charlice Rice, a 30-year-old, high profile realtor from Wicker Park in Chicago, was involved in a long term abusive relationship with married father of three, church deacon, and police detective Douglass Smith. Smith forced his way into her apartment, assaulted Charlice which resulted in her jaw being broken, blunt trauma to the head and body. He sexually assaulted her. She had to go to the hospital. His reason for the assault was because she was leaving him to move to D.C. without telling him. He said the fight was mutual even though he was found in her apartment with bloody knuckles. He claimed the sex was consensual.

Karen found another article about Doug's conviction and sentencing. Doug had lost everything. Even though he maintained his innocence, he was found guilty of the assault and the rape. He was sentenced to 15 years in prison. Charlice did not attend trial. Her mother Charlene testified but Charlice was mentally unable to attend or attest. He was convicted without her testimony.

Shaking her head Karen said, "This woman is trouble." *I have got to talk to Peaches.*

She picks up her phone and calls her friend Peaches.

Peaches answers, "Hey girl!"

"Hey girl! Whatchu doin'?" Code switching. That's what she does when she gets with Peaches. "We need to talk. In person."

"Girl what is going on wit' chu? I'm home cleaning and washing clothes. Just getting ready for work Monday. You good?" Peaches asks.

"No. I need some friendly advice."

"Well come on over girl. I will see you when you get here. I have a good bottle of Chardonnay in the fridge and a new bottle of Hennessy on the bar." Peaches laughs. "I will see you when you get here."

Karen grabs her laptop. Then scurries around the house looking for her handbag and keys. "Oh here they are." She says as she gets to the sofa. She checks her hair and makeup in the mirror by the door and rushes over to Peaches' house.

I cannot wait to tell Peaches all about Miss Charlice, the realtor homewrecker. "Humph! That high yellow heifer won't wreck my home. I will make sure of that. She will get another beat down from me!"

"There's a feeling within me, begging me to confront and overcome this defeat. But then there are the louder voices creeping in from the shadows of my memory."— Kristina Smeriglio, Tales We Tell The Sky

Chapter II: The Reminiscence

The Past Reminders

"Whew chile!" Peaches exclaims as she flops down on her sofa and throws her leg across the arm of her white sofa. "What is going on with you today Karen?"

Karen walks over into Peaches' kitchen, grabs a wine glass from the rack, the corkscrew from the drawer and the bottle of wine from the fridge. Shaking her head, "Chile, I don't even know where to begin."

Peaches is Karen's only friend. The two of them are an unlikely pair. Peaches grew up in the projects of South East D.C. The infamous Barry Farms to be exact. She graduated from Anacostia High School in the top 10 percentile of her class. Even though Peaches used to love the hustlers and the hustler lifestyle, she was smart enough to know that she needed to go off to college. So she left D.C. and went away to Temple University yet she maintained that hustler mentality.

After she graduated from Temple, she returned to D.C. and landed a good job in the D.C. government with the Community Affairs Department. With her position in the government, Peaches has been able to rub elbows with some of the elite socialites of D.C. Not to mention, Peaches is also the owner of A Touch of Peaches Event Planning. Peaches has planned most of the upscale events for the D.C. elite. Peaches plans All White parties, Vision Board parties, cruises, crab feasts, Tea parties, cotillions and beautillions, along with Go-Go parties. Whatever the bougie can imagine and whatever their expensive budgets allow, A Touch of Peaches Event Planning is the premier planner to choose.

This is one of the main reasons why Karen loves being friends with Peaches. Peaches offers Karen access to all the places where she wants to be. Not to mention nobody else can really put up with Karen.

Karen and Peaches met at one of Peaches' events. Peaches' annual crab feast which raises money for a local youth organization, All Challenges Mastered. Karen was there with one of her former friends. At the event, the two struck up a conversation and found that they had similar interests. One of those being enjoying the life of the elite. They have been friends ever since. Peaches feels sympathy for Karen. Karen supports her events so Peaches considers Karen to be a friend. So, she tries to always make time for Karen since she is going through so much right now.

"Tell me. What happened girl?" Peaches probes.

Karen pours the wine and takes a nice long sip. "Oooh! I needed that." She says as she lays her head back in the big wide forest green chair that Peaches has sitting next to the sofa in front of the sliding glass door of Peaches' luxury condo. "Nothing much. I just had words with Williams's realtor."

"WHAT? William's realtor? Please explain because I am confused."

Karen takes a gulp of her wine. "You're confused? Well, I went to the shop to get my hair done. Lou was almost finished so I texted William to bring me the money to pay her because you know he wants me to look good for him so he comes in to pay for my hair and to make sure it is styled the way he likes it."

"Okay! I remember." Peaches takes a sip of her Hennessy XO waiting for Karen to get to the good part of her story.

"So William walks into the shop. Sees me. Gives me a little smile as he heads towards me. But before he reaches me, he veers off to the right to some random chick sitting in the other chair at Lou's station."

"What Tha Fu..!" Yells Peaches in disbelief. "You are kidding me."

"No ma'am. Forreal. He talkin' and smilin' at her. And she laughin' and smilin' back at him. And I'm just sittin' there watching this exchange in disbelief. Like doesn't he see ME, his beautiful wife, sitting here waiting for him."

"Girl…What did he say because I know you asked him?"

Peaches asks, shaking her head waiting to hear all the tea.

"He said her name was Charlice and she is his realtor. From what I can recall, she is Lou's best friend or something."

"So how did she meet William? Did Lou refer her to him?" Peaches asks.

"That is a good question. I do not know but I sure will ask Lou next week. I have a lot of unanswered questions."

"Go on Karen. I am so sorry. I keep interrupting you." Peaches feels a little remorseful for interrupting Karen's story with her questions. She knows that she is Karen's only friend and Karen needs to get this story off her chest. If she keeps interrupting her, she will have to listen to Karen for hours. And she has an event tomorrow that she needs to finish preparing for. *I'm just going to sit her and let her talk.*

"No problem." Karen responds with an understanding smile. "So William pays the receptionist and we walk out together. He gets in his Jeep and I walk towards my truck. I acted like I was driving off but instead I waited for Miss Charlice to come out."

Peaches interrupts with a burst of laughter. "Ooooh! No you didn't Karen. Then what?"

"I was not sure which car was her's, so I watched her as she headed to a black Mercedes, one of the most expensive ones. I know she ain't making that kind of money. Then I walked over to her and asked her, what was the nature of her business with my husband. She had the nerve to tell me that it was none of my business, while shrugging her eyes. I tried to stay professional with that heifer but she took me there with her little attitude." Karen says, shaking her head with a disgusted look and a snatch back neck.

"Is she cute?" Peaches asks.

"She's a pretty young woman but um... I didn't like her tone so I had to put her in her place." Karen smirks as she took a sip of her wine.

"What did you say?" Peaches asks, looking at Karen side eyed.

"I told her that William is my husband. We are together. We are in love and I have the right to know what business he has with her because my business is his business."

"I know that's right Karen. What did she say to that?" Peaches asks as she sits up waiting to hear the rest of Karen's story.

"She just stood there for a second. Then she said that she was very happy for us." Karen sits up proudly. "I admitted to her that I had made some mistakes and I hadn't been the perfect wife. But I told her, William and I are made for each other. Like our vows say Till Death Do Us Part. Then I turned around, walked away and got in my truck while she continued to stand there with her mouth open."

Peaches burst out laughing. "I love it!" Snapping her fingers in the air, Peaches says, "She bett' not play with my friend and my friend's husband."

Karen laughs. "That's what I was thinking until I talked to William." Getting serious Karen sighed. "He told me to stay away from her. He said she was a nice woman. He forbade me to talk to her like I was his child."

"What?" Peaches asks with a confused expression. "Why?"

"That's what the hell I want to know. So when I got home I hopped on the internet to do a Google search on her because I needed to know who this woman was."

"Oooh Karen!" Peaches was so excited. "What did you find out?"

"She is a real estate agent from Chicago. I think she just moved here. I learned that from the shop. Well when she was in Chicago, she was dating this married police officer who was also heavily involved in his church. When she tried to leave him, he beat her up so badly that she almost died. She was in the hospital for months. There was a huge trial and he got sentenced to prison."

"Oh my goodness." Peaches shocked by what she just learned. "I guess she is here to start a new life."

"Well it looks like she likes married men. It looks like she is chasing after my William. She did or said something to make him so protective of her and talk crazy to me. Do you

30

think she is trying to interfere with my marriage? Do you think William will leave me for her? I cannot lose him now. We have been through so much." Karen jumps up, starts pacing and hitting her left thigh with her left fist.

"Calm down girl. You are reading too much into this. William loves you. You don't have anything to worry about." Speaking calmly, Peaches tries to reassure her friend. "You are just being insecure. What you need to do is focus on Willow and William Jr. William is clearly trying to make this marriage work. Trust your man."

Regaining her composure "You are right Peaches." Breathes deeply. "I need to trust my husband. We have been through so much together. I cannot lose him now. After all, William and I did meet in high school. Remember? I didn't really pay attention to William in high school…"

Here we go again. Peaches thought as Karen starts to retell the story about how she and William met. Peaches has heard the story so many times but she doesn't mind listening. She knows her friend. Karen loves to talk and today she just needs someone to listen.

"In high school, I didn't really pay attention to William even though he was a star on the basketball team and ran outdoor track at McKinley Tech. Remember? I was in a relationship with a different William, but I called him Billy."

"I remember." Peaches mutters as she inhales and takes another gulp of her drink, praying this story will be quick this time around.

"I met Billy in elementary school. A few years after we moved here from Houston. I was in the fifth grade and Billy was in the sixth grade. We went to different schools, but Billy lived near my cousins and I was always at my cousin's house on the weekends, so we were always around each other."

***

Karen was in love with Billy. And she just knew that they would spend the rest of their lives together. However, Billy was not ready for that type of relationship, and he had plenty of girls to prove it. But Karen did not care. She knew that Billy loved her, because he told her so, all the time. Karen and Billy started to have sex when she was thirteen and he was fourteen. The sex began in middle school and continued throughout high school. Billy had girlfriends all over the city, but in Karen's eyes she was number one.

One day while Karen was still in high school, she stopped by Billy's house. His aunt answered the door. She said that Billy was not there, but his car was outside. So Karen walked away, but decided to wait close by his car.

At this time, Billy was in the 12th grade and worked part-time. He had his own car and he was trying to get his own place. He and his mom lived with his mom's sister and her kids. Needless to say, the house was a little too crowded for him and his taste for female guests.

About two hours later Billy comes walking towards his car with a young lady. Karen walked towards Billy and the young lady.

"Hi Billy!" Karen says a little nervous.

"What's up Karen?" Billy asks casually.

"Um, who is this Billy?" She asks, fighting back tears.

Looking Karen up and down proudly, "My friend."

The young lady stops trying to fix her hair, looks at Billy and asks, "Just your friend?"

Billy smirks "Don't do that."

The young lady with an attitude, "Do what?"

"Get in the car, so I can drop you off." Billy yells. Using his finger, he directs her to the car.

The young lady ignored Billy's command, "Who are you?" Talking to Karen.

"I thought I was his girlfriend." Karen responds, quivering. "We have been together since elementary school."

"WHAT?" The young lady screams, looks at Billy and says. "Why didn't you tell me you had a girlfriend? Why have you been leading me on as if I am your girlfriend?"

Billy, fuming, looks at the young lady and says, "Are you really going to believe this crazy ass girl? Look at her. She is delusional. She been in love with me since elementary school. Now do what I told you to do. GET IN THE DAMN CAR!"

The young lady looks over at Karen, while shaking her head feeling dejected. She sucks her teeth and gets in Billy's car.

Billy looks over at Karen. Stares at her with disappointment. He gets in the car with the young lady and drives off leaving Karen standing there alone pounding her left fist to her left thigh.

The tears finally start to trickle down her face.

This was the final straw for Karen. She knew she had to move on. She couldn't continue to let Billy treat her like this. She would not allow another man to abuse her like this. She didn't care how fine he was or how good the sex was.

Karen was so in love with Billy. Even though he was extremely emotionally abusive, she could not shake him. *It was the sex.* She thought. She was addicted to the sex. No one knew that they had been having sex since middle school. She had kept that secret from everyone for all these years.

It wasn't just the sex. In her eyes, Billy was so sexy. Billy had dark course curly hair that she just loved to run her fingers through while they were having sex. His soft pale skin with shades of yellow under-tone, with drops of orange freckles was alluring, and it looked so beautiful laying against her dark chocolate skin. She had it bad.

But somehow she knew that deep inside that he would never come back to her after this. She could tell by the way he looked at her. She needed to move on or at least show him that she didn't need him. "I will show him."

One night Karen and her friends went to a basketball game. Their high school, Dunbar in Northwest D.C., was playing at McKinley Tech. Karen's friends were trying to help her get over Billy so they encouraged her to put her mind on something else.

At the game, one of the players from McKinley was fouled and pushed into the bleachers. He tried to stop his fall but he ended up smack on top of Karen. Their eyes met as his sweaty muscular body laid on top of her. For a moment, Karen didn't mind the fact that a bead of sweat from his forehead had landed right between her eyebrows.

He apologized and asked her if she was okay. She said yes and the game continued but not without quick glances from him and mesmerizing stares from her. She could not take her eyes off of this tall, dark, beautifully chiseled man that she had shared a brief moment with.

After the game, the player came over to Karen.

"Hey! I am so sorry about falling on you. Are you sure you

are okay?" The tall dark player asked.

Blushing Karen replied, "Yes. Thank you. It wasn't your fault. It is all part of the game."

"By the way, my name is William. And you are?"

"Hi William. I know who you are. Everyone in the DMV knows who you are, Mr. William Lime? My name is Karen." She is smiling from ear to ear. *I can't believe his name is William, and I hope he doesn't go by Billy.* Karen thought to herself.

He laughed. "Okay Miss Karen. May I have your number so I can call you later?"

Karen looked in her book bag, tears a sliver of her homework off the corner, and grabbed a pen. She scribbled her name and number on the paper and passed it to William. "Call me later?" She added, as she walked away with her friends hoping that she would hear from him that evening.

For their last year and a half of high school, Karen and William were inseparable. Karen forgot about Billy and focused her attention on William. William was good to her. He made her forget all about Billy for the most part. The sex was just as good. She was happy with William. She had found her soulmate. She trusted.

Karen needed some happiness in her life. She needed a man to love her. She longed for a man to show her love and respect like her father had. Karen believed that she had never shared her story with anyone before William. He made her feel safe; safe enough to share part of her history.

Her father was dead. It was her mother's fault that he was dead. *My dad loved me so much. I hate my mother for what she did. I wish she were dead too.*

Her father had loved her so much and she loved him. He treated her like a princess and kept her on a pedestal. He had shown her how she deserved to be treated.

Karen felt so much guilt for not telling anyone who had killed her father. Yet she did not tell anyone who had killed him. When he died, a part of her died. It was an internal conflict she could never repair. She suffered alone inside because she was afraid. Petrified of the man that had killed him.

Karen's father was gunned down in Houston. So Karen moved to D.C. to stay with one of her mother's family friends. Lordess, Karen's mother, told Oscar, her boyfriend, that Karen ran away. In reality, Karen didn't run away. Lordess sent Karen away because she feared for her daughter's life. While Lordess stayed in contact with Karen, the damage had already been done. Lordess could never repair that relationship, nor could she repair the emotional and mental damage that had been inflicted on her daughter.

***

Peaches notices that Karen has stopped talking. So she breaks the silence. "See that man ain't about to leave you for no homewrecker like that. You all have a special connection that can't easily be broken. Stay focused Karen. Stay focused on the good things. Like this Ivory Soiree girl. You got your outfit yet?"

Karen snaps back into reality. She realized that she was going into that dark place in her mind. She tried her best to stay out of there.

Even though she shared almost everything with Peaches over the years, that dark place was a space for just her. *I have told people that my parents are dead so they both are dead. Dead to me.*

"Girl, I am working on my outfit. I have scheduled an appointment at the Trend Boutique to look at outfits for the party and our Caribbean cruise."

"This is going to be the party of the year. Do you hear me?" Peaches says, punching her fist to her hand.

"I know. That's why I have to make sure my outfit is just right. I cannot have anyone out do me." Karen boasts.

Peaches interrupts her. "Umm, hold up friend." Peaches motions her hands to say, 'Cut that out.' "Except me. You cannot come looking better than the hostess. I have all the Who's Who of the DMV attending this fundraising event. Nothing can ruin this night. With the people who have RSVP'd, there won't be any drama. Only sexy rich people rubbing elbows, bumping booties and writing checks."

Karen laughs. Then she gets somber. "I don't know if I should go on this cruise. What about my marriage? I don't like going without William. He might think I am going to pick up men. My marriage is already in shambles."

"Girl STOP!" Getting angry with Karen. "There you go again. That man loves you. He adores you. He just needed a break. Most men do. Just take this time to enjoy yourself on this Girls Trip. Let William think you are going to go look for a new island man. Let him think you about to hop like a whore to the islands to bend and break your back!"

"You are right." Karen says.

Karen knows Peaches just needs a person to hang out with on the cruise. She knows Peaches really doesn't like the crew that is going on the cruise, but she likes their money enough to put up with anything.

"Trust me. It will be fun." Peaches says. "You deserve a getaway."

"True." Karen looks down at her watch. "Let me get out of here. I have to go pick up the kids. William is coming by the house to see them." She stands up. Puts her wine glass in the sink and heads towards the door. "I will call you later. I have to go home and get cute." Karen looks at herself in the mirror by Peaches' door. She adjusts her hair, checks her makeup and adjusts the lash on her right eye. "I will call you later. Thank you for listening and being my voice of reason. Love you." She heads out the door.

Peaches still laying across the sofa yells back. "Anytime Sweetie. Love you too."

Peaches also knows that she is Karen's only friend. *Who would have thought we would still be hanging out after my crab feast? Karen doesn't really fit in with my crew. God love her. She tries so hard to be one of us.*

"I think if I continue to mold Karen, she could pull off being more like us." Peaches takes the last gulp of her drink and jumps up. "Now I need to go back over my list. Check it twice to make sure that this All White party is the successful event that I know it is going to be. Let me go call Khrystina to make sure she has her outfit together and make sure she has done what I asked her to do." Peaches met Khrystina in college, and they have been friends ever since.

Peaches grabs her cell phone from the table. "Siri, call Khrystina."

"Hello." Khrystina's soft gentle voice says over the phone.

"Khrystina Paine." Peaches yells. "Are you ready for THE Mo Fo White Party of the Year?"

The two friends laugh and continue their conversation about all things White Party.

***

As Karen drives through the streets of D.C, she reflects on her friendship with Peaches. She is so happy to have Peaches as her friend.

Peaches is everything that Karen wants to be. She is popular, charismatic and lives a lavish lifestyle. Sometimes Karen wonders what her life would be like without a husband and children like Peaches. *She gets to do whatever she wants to do, when she wants to do it.*

"Yes, My Touch of Ivory Soiree is going to be a success. I am going to be the Belle of the Ball. All of those socialites will look at me and stare. I'm going to sashay around the room. You know, I will really work the room to get all the men to donate to my charity. Tonight I will make Kent want to leave his wife for me." Karen laughs to herself thinking about how much she will enjoy hosting the gala.

"If you cannot hold me in your arms, then hold my memory in high regard. And if I cannot be in your life, then at least let me live in your heart." — Ranata Suzuki

Chapter III: The Muffled Inquisitorial

The Diligent Inquiry

Keys can be heard jingling at the front door. Then a deep masculine voice calling out, "Hey where is everybody? Helloooo! Willow? Will? Karen?"

William stops by the house a few times a week to check on Karen and the children. William knows that he needs to check on them more often. After his conversation on the phone with Karen, he needs to check the temperature in the household. He knows that Karen has been dealing with some mental health issues so he needed to make sure that his children were safe.

He also needs to check on the mental and physical health of his children. He would hate for them to suffer mentally because of their mother or because of his actions.

He knows what Karen went through as a child and he knows that he has to protect his children at any and all cost.

William walks through the house and encounters Karen in the kitchen. "Did you hear me calling your name?" He asks.

Karen is cooking. She turns from the stove. "No Dear. I did not hear you. I'm cooking. Would you like to join your family for dinner?"

"No, I have already made plans for the evening." William says no because he has plans for later, but he thanks her for the invite.

Willow heard her father calling her names so she ran down the steps but stopped when she overheard the conversation between her mother and father.

Willow had hopes of her parents getting back together. She loves both parents, but she feels sorry for her dad. She feels empathy towards him for everything he has to deal with involving her mom's antics.

Willow, being the oldest, has witnessed first-hand her mother's shenanigans. She has seen her mom talking to herself, crying, yelling at someone but no one was there. She has watched her mom hitting her thigh in frustration. But she has been so afraid to say something because she didn't want anyone to take her mother away. She thought they would put her in a home for the mentally ill and she would never see her mother again. So she suffered in silence.

Willow suspected that her dad knew about her mother. In her mind, she just knew that her dad had seen what she saw but he wanted to ignore it and they never discussed it.

Willow thought about getting her mother help, but did not

know who to turn to. She did not want to tell the school counselors because she was afraid of how they would judge her and her family. She already felt out of place in that school. No matter how much money her dad had, she would never fit in at Sidwell Friends. It was half white, and the other half, all others. Her dad was paying over 40 thousand a year for her and her brother to attend this 'prestigious' school. *Prestigious to who?* She thought.

Willow could tell that her dad was stressed about paying all the bills and still having to make sure they were good in school and at home. She felt his burden and she knew that her mom's antics did not help him relieve any stress.

Willow was a very observant child. She recognized that none of the parents at Sidwell Friends cared for her mother; it was because of Karen's personality. Karen always wanted to fit in with whatever group she was around and she just tried too hard, which just turned out to be a disaster and made the parents isolate Karen, William and sometimes Willow and Will, Jr.

While in the kitchen, Karen is standing in front of the stove pretending to focus on stirring the sauce for the spaghetti. She is actually watching William out of the corner of her right eye. William is sitting at the table texting and smiling at his phone.

"How is house hunting going, dear?" Karen asks gently. "When are you going to let us see our beautiful new home? When will we be able to move in? I am so excited to start this new chapter of our life."

William ignores Karen. He looks away from his phone and looks down at his watch trying to figure out how long he has been waiting for the kids to come downstairs.

"Yes, true. This is a nice safe neighborhood but a house in the Bethesda/ Chevy Chase area would be great. I am sure that there are plenty of beautiful homes out there. The area conveniently has all of the high end stores that I adore. That area is also close to Sidwell Friends." She pauses to look over at William. "The kids wouldn't have to transfer schools. The location is perfect."

William stops pretending to ignore his wife. He looks over at her as she is standing there smiling and unbothered. "Karen." He says softly.

Karen cuts William off, "If we do move too far, we have to make sure Willow has a new car to get back and forth to school. Yes, Chevy Chase it is. Tell that Chartice woman that we prefer the Chevy Chase area."

William calmly utters, "The house hunting is going well. I have decided to buy a house in the Upper Marlboro Largo area of Maryland. When the time comes, Willow should have her own car to drive to school on the days when she is coming from MY house. By the way, her name is CharLICE not CharTICE as you put it."

"Oh okay! Her name really isn't that important. All that matters is that she does what we pay her to do." Karen flips her hand toward William as if to say who cares. "Upper Marlboro? Hmmm! I don't know too much about that area. Isn't that the hood? How far is that from the kids' school? Will it be too far for me to take them to school? What upscale shops are in that area?" Karen starts setting the table for four people not making eye contact with William.

William is sitting in awe just listening to her. He has no intention of allowing her to move into his Upper Marlboro home. He wants Charlice to move in with him. He knows that he and Charlice can have a wonderful life together.

Once he gets back on his feet, he wants to purchase another house in the D.C., maybe the southwest or southeast area. *A house close to the water would be perfect. I know Charlice can find the perfect property for us.*

Karen stopped talking for a second when she realized that William was just staring at her. She was not going to let up about moving into their new house. She knew William. She just knew he was not going to let his family life go that easy. After all, he had been working so hard to put the pieces back together. He pays all of the bills for the household. She does not have to pay for ANYTHING. *Humph! He's not going anywhere.*

William wants Karen to keep the house in Tenley Circle so the children will be close to their school. *She needs to stay here especially after we almost lost this house because of her actions. I was finally able to catch up with the mortgage and able to pay cash for my new home in Largo.*

Besides, now is not a good time to sell. Karen would lose her mind if she found out that I bought this new house.

William realizes that Karen has stopped talking. "Oh what did you say?" He asks.

Karen grits her teeth because he isn't listening and she has to repeat all of her questions. "I asked about Upper Marlboro."

William, a little irritated, declares, "I said the house hunt is going well. Charlice has shown me several houses in Upper Marlboro. There will be plenty of space for Willow and Will, so no need to worry about that." William did not want Karen to know that he had actually purchased the house.

Charlice stays overnight often because Lou's family is there at the house. William knows that Charlice loves the peace and quiet she gets when she is over his house. William loves having Charlice at his home; their home together. *How am I going to break this to Karen? Slowly. The kids? How do I tell them about Charlice?*

William's plan has always been to walk away from Karen slowly because he knows how fragile she is. But now he feels a sense of urgency because he really wants to be with Charlice. He knows that Charlice would make him much happier than Karen. The past few days with Charlice have been like a breath of fresh air for him. He cannot believe how quickly he has fallen for this woman. Charlice and Karen are such different women.

Karen was so focused on the "who you know, I know you, you know me crowd" and wanted to be close to the streets. She wanted to be in the spotlight. On the other hand, Charlice did not care about the crowd and streets of the city, because she really did not know anyone. She just wanted to be discreet. Live a peaceful, quiet life. William liked the fact that Charlice did not really know anyone besides Lou.

Willow was still on the steps listening to her parents. When she heard her dad interrupt her mom and say, "Let me go talk to the kids before I leave. Then he asked, "What do they have planned for Thursday?"

Willow hurried and tipped toed back up the stairs into her room. To her surprise, Will Jr. was in her room. He startled her.

"Umm…What are you doing in my room?" Willow asks.

Will just looks at her, not sure how to answer the question.

William goes upstairs to talk to the kids and Karen is still talking to him about their new house.

When William gets upstairs, he finds both kids in Willow's room. "Hey guys! Didn't y'all hear me calling your names?" He opens his arms looking for hugs.

Will runs over to his dad and gives him a big welcoming hug. "Dad, I'm so happy to see you. I missed you."

"I missed you too buddy." William hugs his son back.

"Willow?" William reaches out for her to join their hug.

Willow slowly blinks her eyes but then walks over into her dad's arms. She has missed her dad but she feels a little anger towards him for leaving them with their mom.

William steps back and looks at his kids. "It seems like forever since I have seen you two."

Willow squints her eyes with curiosity. "We just saw you last week dad. Remember?"

"Oh yeah! I forgot. Give me another hug." William laughs and pulls his kids into his body tightly. He misses his children so much. He needs to spend more time with them.

"Listen guys. Thursday night. We have a date. The three of us."

"Yahhh! Where are we going?" Will Jr. asks.

"Take a guess."

"Sky Zone?" Will Jr. yells out.

Shaking his head. William replies, "No."

Excited Will Jr. starts calling out, "The zoo? Six Flags? Jump Zone?"

William keeps shaking his head saying, "No! No! No!"

Will Jr. continues to name places and William keeps telling him no.

All of a sudden, Willow yells out, "OH MY GAH! JUST TELL US! WHERE ARE YOU TAKING US? DANG!"

William and Will Jr. look at each other then look at her.

"I am taking us to the circus. How does that sound?"

While Willow shakes her head in antipathy, Will Jr. jumps up and down excited.

William ignores Willow's reaction. "Oh good! We are going to have so much fun. Perhaps we can make an entire weekend out of it. You two can spend the weekend with me and we can go shopping at Tyson's Corner in the morning. Wouldn't that be fun?"

While her brother is still jumping up and down with excitement, Willow looks at her dad side-eyed. Then asks, "How are we going to stay with you and you ain't got nowhere to stay? You living in a room at your friend's house. I'm not staying over there."

William laughs, "Don't worry about all that ma'am. Just know that I have a nice comfortable place for you to lay your pretty little head."

"Oh really?"

"Yes, ma'am. I have made arrangements because I want to spend more time with you and your brother since I am not living in this house with you all."

Willow looking confused. "So you aren't planning on

moving back in with us? But mom said…"

Grabbing Willow's hands and looking into her eyes, William says, "Willow I am so sorry that your mom has told you all that I was moving back in with you all. I am not sure what I am going to do right now. But just remember that your mom and I love you and your brother more than anything. But we cannot make you two happy if we are not happy. Do you understand?"

Will Jr. could care less. He shakes his head accepting what his dad is saying.

On the other hand, Willow has questions because she does not understand. "What I understand is that you and mom are married. We are a family. I know mom does some things that might be odd to most people but you're her husband and you need to help her. 'Till death do you part?"

William is taken aback by what Willow just said. *She must have been listening to her mother.* "Yes Willow. You are correct. However, people grow apart and people change. Your mom and I have both changed. We need time to heal. This time apart does not mean that I do not love your mother. It means that I have some things to work on and so does she. So now we need to continue to make the most of this as a family. At least you will have your own bedroom. You can decorate the room anyway you want. How does that sound?"

"Okay dad!" Willow concedes. "I will work with you as

you work on yourself and mom works on herself. Both of y'all need therapy."

William burst out laughing at his daughter's diagnosis. He hugs her and grabs Will's hand as he leads them downstairs for dinner.

In the meantime, Karen was still in the kitchen talking. She didn't even realize that William had walked out of the kitchen. She is having a conversation as if William is still there.

"William, why are you keeping her in suspense about our new home? I know you want me to be surprised but this anticipation is just becoming unbearable."

William has always surprised Karen with lavish gifts and exotic romantic trips. Surprising her with a new house was nothing out of the ordinary for him.

Karen believed that William knew she had improved as a wife and mother. *I just know he is ready to give me the second chance I need, want and deserve.*

"Well," Karen says. "I will start packing up the house in the next couple of weeks. Better yet, I will hire a moving company to come, pack and move. I will give you 30 days. The house should be ready then, knowing you."

William and the children enter the kitchen. They stop at the entrance to the kitchen when they realize that Karen is talking to someone.

She pops the question again, "When will the house be ready, dear?"

The children sit down at the table and William steps out of the kitchen to answer a call on his cell phone. He decides not to answer Karen.

When he comes back in the kitchen, to announce that he will be leaving, Karen asks, "So what time will you be picking us up for the circus on Thursday?"

Who told her we were going to the circus? William looks at the kids and then looks at her, and says, "Who said you were coming?" He now decides to answer.

Shocked by his question, Karen laments, "We are a family. We go everywhere together. You remember don't you? That's how it has always been, and that is how it will always be. You just need more time to figure out what we are going to do differently as a family, so we don't have to separate the family again. It has really caused a toll on the children since you left. I told you that you didn't have to leave. I told you we could figure it out. You said that you would never leave me. You said you would always be there for me. Now, you decide to change your mind. What did I do so bad that you would want to get up and leave your family?" She breaks out in deep sobs.

Then continues. "Your son needs you here in the house with him. He is too young to understand and I am not sure I can explain all of this. This is too much for me to handle.

You could have given me a heads up that you would be leaving. But no, instead, you just packed up and left. "Karen pauses again to muster up more tears and to look at Williams's reaction out the side of her napkin.

Gently, William says, "Karen, I told you I was going to leave if you didn't change your ways and get better. You chose not to listen. You chose not to change. You thought you could continue to walk all over me because you know how I feel about marriage and the vows I took. You took me for granted, Karen. I am tired, Karen."

William pauses to check the children's reactions because he knows that they should not be having this conversation in front of them but at the same time he realizes that they need to hear this.

"You were not always like this. Why did you change Karen? You loved the simple things in life, then you met some new friends and you went buck wild with the spending. Why do you feel the need to prove to people that you have material things? Why is that so important to you now? We have kids to raise. We have kids that provide a better life for. Better than what you and I had. Instead, you want to buy Louis, Gucci, YSL and whoever else you think is going to impress your friends."

Will Jr. is eating his dinner not paying attention. Willow has her head down playing with her food and absorbing all of the information from her parents back and forth.

"What you fail to realize is that those people are not your friends. They are pretentious individuals who are trying to fill a void. Why can't you see that? This is why I stop going to those events with you. They all want to know how much money you make, where you work, where you live, what kind of vehicle you drive, and the dumb stuff that doesn't matter. They want to outdo somebody, but outdo who? The person they think has more than them? This is the lifestyle that you want for our children? I am trying to get away from all of that. None of it matters if you're not happy, and I am not happy with you or the decisions you have made."

Karen wipes her tears, "You may not be happy now William Lime, but you will be when we are all back under one roof. I understand what you are saying, but you don't understand me, and what I am dealing with. You never really supported me in anything."

Willow looks up; looks at her dad. Then looks at her mom. Shakes her head and puts her head back down to finish playing with her food. She cannot believe her mother just said that to her dad. *I cannot wait for him to go off on her.*

William can't believe the words that are coming out of Karen's mouth. *This woman is more delusional than I thought. Does she hear anything she is saying?*

William knew that this process was not going to be easy. At this point, he had no idea how he was going to end this situation. This was more than he bargained for.

"Listen Karen, I don't want to argue with you anymore nor do I want to continue this conversation in front of the kids. I would really like to spend more time with my kids. I have not seen them for a while because of my work hours, their activities and this separation. Could you at least let me have some time alone with them? Please, Karen?"

"I don't think it is necessary for you to spend time alone with the children." Karen says as she has gained her composure. "Since we are working on getting back together. There is nothing wrong with us going to the circus as a family. Yes, this would be the perfect opportunity for us to bond."

"Sorry Karen." William says, I didn't buy a ticket for you. "I honestly didn't think you wanted to go with us."

Damn. William thought. *How do I convince her that this is not the event for our family? I already invited Charlice so she could meet the kids.*

Karen knew William was just saying that to make her mad. *William does not have it in his heart to leave me out.*

"No worries, Dear. I will purchase my own ticket. Please make sure there is money in the account."

Willow jumps in the conversation, "Mom, you are being so selfish. We never get to spend time with dad anymore. Why can't you just let us have this day with him? You ruin everything."

"Watch your tone with your mother, Willow." William reminds her.

"Dad. You know I am right. You just asked to spend some time with us and she wants to come. Do you really want to go to the circus or do you just want to be stuck up under dad? You're the reason dad left. He is tired of you. He is tired of you talking to yourself. He is tired of you spending his money frivolously. We are all tired of YOU."

Will Jr. chimes in, "I'm not tired of you mommy. I love you."

"SHUT UP WILL! NO ONE ASKED YOU. You need to ask your mother why you are so light skinned."

"That is enough Willow." Karen interrupts with tears in her eyes. "You have said enough hurtful things to me today."

Willow storms off up the stairs and to her room slamming the door behind her. Karen and William decide that they would let her have time to herself.

"So what time should we be ready for the circus?" Karen asks.

William knew he had created a monster. He didn't know how he was going to get out of this situation. He has always provided a thousand percent. In the beginning, it was because of the relationship. Karen was a good woman but things started to change once she started having kids.

William had to continue with the support because Karen

had become accustomed to the lifestyle. William had always been basic. He never liked the flashy stuff and materials because he felt like it drew too much attention. He didn't like that kind of attention. He was the opposite of Karen.

On the other hand, Karen loved the material attention. She wanted people to see that she had made it. She wanted people to know that she could have whatever she wanted. She wanted people to know that her husband provided everything and anything that she desired.

William stood up. Kisses Will Jr.'s forehead and says, "I will see you in the morning buddy. Karen, have the kids ready by 4."

Then he walks out the front door. He takes a deep breath to release some of the pressure that he felt in that house. Something tells him to turn around. He turns around and looks up. Willow is standing in the window with her hand pressed against the glass. William smiles at his daughter, blows her a kiss and whispers, "I love you!"

Willow rolls her eyes and pulls the curtains shut.

When he looks down, he notices Karen standing in the window waving. She is so excited. He turns his head back towards the driveway. He takes another deep breath and walks to his truck. He sits in his truck for a second to clear his mind. Then he thinks. *It is time for me to head to my new home to meet up with my new woman. I cannot wait to see her.* Willow's actions at the window made him feel really bad but he was optimistic about the future. *Tomorrow is a new day. We will have a wonderful time together. Willow, Will, Charlice and I...my new little family.*

"All inquiries carry with them some element of risk."— Carl Sagan, Broca's Brain: Reflections on the Romance of Science

Chapter IV: The Obligation

The Moral Bondage

William pulls up in front of the Tenley home to pick up the kids for the circus. He purchased four tickets. William asked Charlice to attend the circus with him and the children. That way their initial meeting with Charlice would be in a happy place, a public place to avoid any awkwardness.

William knows that Charlice will just love the kids once she meets them in person. He envisions what life would be like in their new house. *Charlice would be like a second mom to Will and Willow. She and Willow will become friends. I know they love their mother but they need another woman as head of household. Someone ambitious and successful like Charlice.*

William thinks for a moment. *Am I moving too fast? Should I slow down a bit? I'm not divorced. I haven't even filed separation papers or divorce papers. I haven't even told my wife that I want to move on. Am I being selfish or cautious?*

While sitting in his truck waiting for the kids, he texts Karen to let her know that he was there. He asks her to send the kids out. He also texts Charlice to let her know that he is picking up the children now.

William is nervous and excited. He is nervous about the children meeting Charlice and he is excited about spending time with the children at the circus.

As he is sitting in front of the house still waiting, smiling he thinks *I will have to get up extra early to take Willow and Will J to school Monday morning after our long family weekend.*

William sends Charlice a picture of the ticket sections so she knows where they will be sitting just in case she arrives later or before they arrive.

Charlice texts William. "Received. I will see you shortly."

The circus starts at 7 o'clock. Charlice looks down at her watch. It was now around 3 o'clock. She realizes that she has a couple of transactions that she needs to close out before leaving the office.

She is excited about meeting William's kids. When she was with Doug, her ex-boyfriend, she was never able to meet his children. *His wife would never have allowed that to happen.*

William got startled by the tap at his window. It was Karen and the children so he unlocked the door so the kids could hop in and they could be on their way.

Karen hops into the front passenger seat and the kids get in the back seat. Karen is smiling ear-to-ear. "Hey Dear!" She turns around into the back seat and reminds the kids to buckle up.

William is in shock. He had no idea that Willow had told Karen that she could go with them. "Karen. Where are you going? I told you yesterday that I did not have a ticket for you. You need to get out."

Karen starts laughing. She just knew that William bought her a ticket to go with them. Willow told her that dad had four tickets. *Who else would he have bought a ticket for? Why wouldn't he want me to go?* She is the mother. He is the father. They are a family. *Plus, he loves his family and he wants them all to be together.* She knew that this was one of the steps William was taking to get his family back together and on the right track. She knew this time; she would not mess up this perfect opportunity. "Dear," She says smiling like a Cheshire cat, "you said we were going to the circus. Willow said you bought me a ticket. She said you had four tickets."

William turns around and looks at Willow like 'Explain?'

Willow chimes in, "Yea dad. I saw that you bought four tickets. I thought maybe you were just joking with mom last night so I told her about the ticket so she wouldn't be so upset."

William just shakes his head. "You shouldn't have done that Willow."

Karen knew her husband was on the fence about her and the relationship. "It's okay, Dear. I went online and purchased another ticket, just in case." She was going to be there with her family regardless. Besides, the kids would want their mother right there with them during this family fun time.

"Karen, the ticket was not for you. I had planned on being with the kids." He shakes his head in frustration. "This ticket is not for you." He tries to talk her out of going but she is adamant about going.

Karen just knew that William was not bold enough to have another woman around her kids this soon in the game. *He wouldn't bring no woman around my kids when we are trying to work things out. Would he?* "We are going to have an AMAZING family day at the circus, kids. We haven't done this in a while. Thank you William for coming up with this idea." Karen pulls down the mirror on the visor in front of her and starts applying some more makeup and fixing her hair.

Willow and William wanted their family back together because they were used to a two parent home so they were excited to be going on this family outing with both of their parents. The only unhappy person was William.

He tried to call Charlice to make an excuse for her not to

come. She did not answer. *Damn.* He thought. *She must already be there. I don't know how I am going to fix this.*

William has mixed feelings. He does not want the kids to be affected by the separation because he knows how it affected him as a child. *Foster care taught me how important it is for a child to have a stable family. I would never want Willow or Will J. to feel like I did. I will find a way to make this up to Charlice. Hopefully, she will understand.*

***

Charlice arrives at the circus excited and nervous to meet the children. Hopefully, her soon to be step children. *I hope they like me.*

Charlice tells the staff at the gate that William has her ticket. She tries to call him but he doesn't answer. The staff let her go through.

This is her first time at the circus. She had no idea it would smell like a zoo. It makes sense though with all of the animals.

Charlice was in awe as she walked deeper into the dark arena circle. It was just like she had imagined it to be. The huge ring in the center of the arena, surrounded by seats filled with anxious children. In the center of the ring, stands a tall slender African American man wearing one of the most elaborate purple and gold satin suits that she has ever seen. His suit and matching hat were bedazzled with gold and purple sequins, rhinestones and glitter. He is standing on what appeared to be a floating pedestal, *No handlebar mustache, humph?*

All lights are on him and only him. He stretches left arm out and then his right arm. The crowd goes wild in anticipation as to what he is going to do next. The Ringmaster snaps his fingers and the lights go on like an explosion and a herd of beautiful white horses came galloping out from the big red curtains. The last horse is ridden by a woman wearing a sparkling white and gold costume that looks almost like a bathing suit. She begins doing tricks and flips with the horses. For a moment, Charlice stands there watching until she is bumped by a small child who is trying to get a better look at the lady acrobat. She almost forgot she was supposed to be looking for William and the kids. Her nerves start to kick in again as she gets closer to the section where William and the kids are sitting.

When she gets to the section there is a sudden flash of lights from above the ring. That is when she sees William, the children and Karen. The smile on her face fades. Then hurt and anger start to form. Memories of Doug, her ex-boyfriend, start to fill her mind. *Is this a repeat of my relationship with Doug? I never met Doug's kids because of his wife.*

She really didn't have to deal with all of this family drama when she was dealing with Doug. Doug always kept his family life separate. She never met his kids. So now she starts thinking that Doug really had no plans for leaving his wife. *Four years and I never met anyone from Doug's family. Humph? Why didn't I think about that before? I wasted four years of my life. If I had made a decision to leave Doug four years ago, maybe I would not be here now. I would be with an available man that knows how to treat me.*

Why did William ask me to come, if Karen was going to be here? This is some bullshit. I refuse to do this again. I refuse to take a backseat to another wife. This is not what William explained to me. He said that they were not together. Why are they sitting here at the circus like a cute little family? Charlice doesn't know what to think.

She notices that William is not sitting with Karen. The children are sitting in the middle, and William and Karen are sitting on opposite ends. He doesn't look very happy. He just looks like he is there.

Charlice wonders if she should go over to William. Or should she just pretend to be at the circus by herself? No, then she would be looking crazy. She notices that William keeps looking around almost like he is looking for her. Like he is expecting someone. Her?

Maybe William wants her and Karen to meet. Maybe he told Karen about me. I wonder how Karen feels about me. Does Karen know that William and I have future plans of moving in together? I have so many questions. I am just confused.

While Charlice was standing in his view wondering what the heck was going on, William was sitting with Karen and the children contemplating what he was going to tell Charlice. Every now and then he would look around to see if she was approaching them. He did not want to be too obvious because he wants to enjoy his time with the kids, in spite of Karen ruining his plans.

Charlice should have been here by now. She must have seen us. I know she is pissed. William decides, *now I'm going to have to tell Karen about Charlice. I love Charlice. I have not felt this way about another woman ever. When will I tell Karen? How will I tell Karen? And the kids? How will I tell the kids? Ugh! Why did I make this situation so difficult? I deserve to be happy. Dammit! I am going to tell Karen this evening.*

William looks over at his children enjoying the circus. Then he looks over at Karen who is looking at him smiling. With a feeling of distaste, William looks over to his left and he sees Charlice standing there glaring at him with hate in her eyes.

Charlice's eyes locked with William's. Before she knew it, some kids bumped past her and broke her eye contact with William. The little boy's red drink spilled all over her jeans. When she looked back over at William and his family, she noticed that he was no longer looking at her. Perhaps he had not noticed her, or did he see her and choose to ignore her.

I have had enough. Charlice is pissed so she decides to leave and go back to the office to work. Plus, she had a lot to think about.

As she is walking towards the top of the arena, a flash of light bursts through the crowd and at that moment, William finally sees Charlice. "I will be right back." He says before Karen can even ask where he is going. He darts out of the arena to catch Charlice.

William calls out to Charlice. She hears him but she keeps walking. He catches up to her and grabs her arm. "Charlice, do you hear me calling you?"

Charlice, pissed answers, "Yes, I hear you calling me. Did you see my text messages? Did you see my repeated calls? What the hell is going on here William?"

"Charlice, I am sorry. Karen just jumped in the truck when I went to pick up the kids. Willow saw the four tickets and assumed that I bought the fourth ticket for her mother so SHE invited her."

"William, you embarrassed me. You hurt me. You made me feel less than a woman. Less than your woman. You made me feel like your whore." Charlice is getting loud and people are starting to stare.

William pulls her to the side. He tries to speak. Charlice interrupts him.

"Remember I told you about my ex Doug? I told you about

that relationship. He was married. He did not tell me at the beginning but when I found out I was too far into the relationship. I was already in love with him. He never brought me around his kids. I had to watch him and his wife sitting in church together with their kids like a big happy family." Charlice stops yelling for a few seconds to keep herself from crying.

William wraps his arms around her to give her and holds her head tight to his chest. He leans down and whispers in her right ear, "Charlice, I apologize. I never meant to hurt you. I promise it will never happen again and I promise that I will make it up to you one way or another. I am not Doug. I promise you I am not him."

William and Charlice are standing in a small secluded area on the side of the concession stand. Karen, who decided to see where her husband was, spots William but decides to go over to the concession stand. She sees the end of William's embrace with another woman.

Karen waits in line at the concession stand and orders two sodas and two large bags of popcorn for her family to share. She watches William talking to someone trying to see who the woman is. She thinks to herself, *William is so friendly. That woman seems upset about something. She looks kinda familiar. Oh hold up! Is that... Is that the real estate agent? That Chartice woman is a stalker. She must be stalking us. Oh my goodness! She is just everywhere.*

Karen pays for her concessions and walks past them. Stops

and says, "Hey Dear! You are missing the show. Take care of this business and come sit with your family." She looks Charlice up and down, with a little sarcastic grin and proceeds to walk back to their seats.

Charlice looks back at William snatches her arm away from him and leaves him standing there calling her name.

She sits in her car for a minute to clear her head before she gets on the road. She looks at her phone. She has four missed calls from William and one text saying 'We need to talk.' "Humph!"

She drives off and heads to her office to finish up some more paperwork and to compile some listings for clients.

When Charlice arrives, Lori, the receptionist, is still at the office. Charlice asks, "Umm! What are you still doing here? I thought I was the only one who would be the crazy person in the office this late."

Lori laughs, "No you are not the only crazy person in the office. Sometimes we have clients that fly in from other countries, from different time zones so I have to be here to greet them and make sure they are taken care of, such is the case this evening. We have clients here from Japan tonight. I don't mind. I get paid overtime and it isn't that often enough to ruin my entire love life." Lori looks at Charlice. "The question is, "What are YOU doing here? You are the one who left here for a hot date."

"Girl!" Charlice begins because she really needs to talk to

someone. "It was a disaster. I have been seeing this man. He has been separated from his wife for a while so we have been taking things slow." Charlice decides she would not tell Lori everything because she does not know her that well. Charlice doesn't want her personal business spread around the office so soon.

Lori is all ears because she loves a good story. "Um hum! I know this story girl oh so well. Go ahead. Tell me all about it."

Charlice continues, "Well, since we have been seeing each other for a few weeks, he asks me if I would feel comfortable meeting his children for the first time at the circus and the four of us; let me repeat. The FOUR of us would spend the rest of the weekend together. He really wants me to get to know the kids. He is not with his wife. He is done. He wants me to move in with him. Blah! Blah! Blah!"

"I know the Blah! Blah!" Lori laughs.

"Right, right!" Charlice suppresses a fake laugh. "So I take my happy ass to the circus. I scurry my way through the crowd to get to where he is sitting with the kids. Low and behold, he is sitting with his wife and kids. I am counting four people. Don't I make five? So what the hell is going on? So now he ain't responding to my texts. He's not calling me. He's not answering my calls. So now I am pissed. THEN this little blonde haired kid spills his red drink all over my jeans so now I am beyond ready to leave because I was about to confront him in front of the wife and kids. That little blonde haired boy must have been a sign from God for me to go home."

Lori burst out laughing. "God WILL give you a sign before you do something you may regret."

"True! He will do that. So I am leaving and I hear him calling my name and I refuse to turn around. Next thing I know I feel someone snatching my arm pulling me back. It is him. We are standing in the middle of the lobby by the concession stand. I am getting loud and he is apologizing so we step to the side to talk calmly."

Lori, engulfed in the story asks, "Why was his wife there? Did he explain why?"

"According to him, his daughter saw that he had four tickets so she assumed that the fourth ticket was for their mother. He is begging me to forgive him. He is telling me that he is nothing like my ex-boyfriend. He would never hurt me. He gives me this big warm hug. We are both calm. We are about to come to a resolution. I am about to give in and forgive him.

Then his wife steps up and tells him to come back with his family once he finishes his business. She gave me the up and down look with a stupid grin like 'See my husband is with me.' I wanted to smack him and her, so I left him standing there and I came here to finish my work. And now I don't know what to do. I don't have time for this foolishness." Charlice throws her hands up as if to say I give up.

Lori shakes her head, "Now I am going to play devil's advocate. Did you really listen to him? If he told you to come meet the kids, why would he bring his wife? Did you really give him a chance? You just walked out and left him there. You know how us women are. She was trying to make you think they are together. Come on now. You know the game we play. You know the Make a Bitch Jealous Game? You let her beat you in that battle?"

"Oh my gosh!" Charlice thinks you are right. "Damn! I hate to lose too. Okay! She got this one but that will be her one win."

"Okay! So what is the plan? How are you going to fix this? How are you going to win over the kids?" Lori asks.

Charlice looks down, "This is going to sound bad but I have to be honest with myself. I don't really want a relationship with his kids. I mean I don't want to act like we are a big happy family. Then they go back home to their mother. I mean I am going to be nice to them but I'm not going to their mother. If he and I are living together, the kids can come spend the night, spend some weekends. Then they need to go home. I am not going to their games and concerts. I am not ready for that. They ain't my kids. I'm sorry."

"No judgment Charlice. I understand but did you tell him

that? Does he know how you feel?"

"We never talked about it. He just said he wants me to meet his kids. This is all new to me. I never met my last boyfriend's children. His wife wasn't having that. What if I don't like his kids? What if his kids don't like me? What happens if he and I have our own kids? Does he even want more kids? I have so many questions. Maybe I should just leave him alone and be single."

"All of your questions are valid," says Lori. "But first you need to forgive him, talk to him and let things happen. If it is meant to be, then it will work out. Forgive the man. It sounds like you really care about him."

"Lori you are so right. I am just going to let things happen. I will reach out to him and forgive him. Thank you."

"You are so welcome. Anytime." Lori starts to laugh. "Well if things don't work out with this one, you can always forget about him and date that fine ass chocolate man, Mr. Lime that you sold a house to. Ooh, that man is fine."

Charlice busts out laughing, "No thank you! Bye Girl. I am going to my office to get some work done. If you are not here when I get back down, I will see you in the morning."

"It's just a thought. Have a good evening, Charlice"

Charlice heads up the steps to her office. *If Lori only knew Mr. Lime is the man. I will let her know the truth once we are married.* She laughs to herself.

***

The drive home from the circus was a quiet one. Or at least it seemed that way to Karen because William wasn't talking to her. But come to think of it, he didn't talk to her at the circus either. *Is he mad? But why? We had such a wonderful family outing.*

Karen wanted to have a conversation with William at the circus to follow-up on the conversation at the house, but she was sitting too far away to talk to him.

When they arrived at the house, the kids hugged their dad and jumped out of the truck. The kids already decided that they were going to stay home for the weekend instead of going with their father. After the kids got out of the truck, Karen remained. William attempted to ignore her because he was angry about her ruining his weekend.

"Good night kids! I hope you had a great time. Love you! See you next week." William says as he turns to drive off. William did not want to talk to Karen, he really wanted to spend time and enjoy his children. He knew this was pretty hard for them but Karen stole that from him.

He knows what Karen went through as a child and he does not want to cause her additional heartache so he knows that any conversation that he has with her will be bad. Before she can say anything, looking straight ahead at the window, he says, "Karen, I cannot talk to you right now. We will continue this conversation on another day. Just take care of Willow and Will J. Yes, I am angry with you. I do not want to say anything that I will regret. Please get out of my truck. I will talk to you next week."

Karen stays quiet. She realizes that there is no need for her to try to talk to him. So she gets out of the truck. Before she closes the door, she says, "Thank you Will for the lovely evening with our family. We had a great time. I will talk to you next week. I love you. Do you love me? Do you still love me William?"

William looks at her. Hesitating, he shakes his head yes.

Beaming, she closes the door.

He drives away.

Karen stands there satisfied with his answer to her question. *He loves me.* She thinks to herself. *I knew it.* Karen walks in the house even more determined to work on her failing marriage.

William drives off hoping that he did not make a mistake by telling Karen that he loves her. *She is going to think that we have a chance to be together. I have to tell her the truth. I need to be honest with her but I have no idea how to do that. Nothing I do convinces her that I don't want this marriage anymore. Now that I have met Charlice I am really torn.*

William's phone alerts him that he has a message. He looks at his truck's dashboard and sees that he has a message from Charlice. The message reads, 'We need to talk. I will meet you at the house.'

He responds, 'I am on my way.'

William pulls up in front of his house. Right next to Charlice's car. He is so elated that she is here. As he is walking up the walkway, he is thinking that he has so much to tell her. He just wants to hold her tight and let her know that he is sorry.

He opens up the door and notices the aroma of something that smells delicious. He puts his keys down on the table by the front door and heads towards the kitchen. There he sees Charlice standing over the stove stirring a pot on the stove. She is wearing one of his big black t-shirts and some tight gray leggings that grip every curve of her lower body.

She looks up at him and gives a faint smile. He knows that she is okay. He walks up behind her. Slides his arms around her waist and begins kissing her neck. She lifts her arms up and reaches back to stroke the back of his neck. At the same time, she is arching her back and rubbing her behind along the front of his pants and he starts moving his hips to match the motion of her body.

William then slides his hands up under her shirt, grabs her breast and begins caressing them as he pulls her into his body. As they grind in rhythm, he starts sucking her ear and whispers, "I have something to tell you."

Staying with the rhythm and stroking the back of his neck, Charlice moans, "Yass, what is it that you need to tell me?"

William slowly removes one hand from her breast and slides his hand down into the front of her leggings which causes them to roll down slightly. Charlice jumps a little as his warm hand finds a comforting place between her legs. William takes his other hand and with one swoop his pants come down, her leggings fall to the floor and Charlice finds herself leaning on the counter while William grips her left shoulder and begins pumping long deep strokes of his manhood into her. Charlice is screaming with pleasure.

William then pulls her down on the kitchen floor and climbs on top of her and continues to give himself to her. His strokes are deliberate, strong and intense. Charlice and William have made love before but never like this.

He starts to talk to her as he is administering stroke after stroke, "Charlice, I have something to tell you."

She can't answer.

William whispers, "I'm sorry for today. Do you forgive me?"

She nods yes.

"I will never hurt you. I won't let anyone come between me and you. Do you understand?"

Charlice screams in pleasure, "Yes! Yes!"

Continuing the rhythm that they are creating, William grabs her face, "I love you, Charlice."

"I…love…you…too, William."

They climax simultaneously and just lay there on the damp kitchen floor.

William lays there thinking. *Got her! I am going to make this work. I have to tell Karen. I can't worry about Karen and her mental health. She is not my problem. I need to help her move on.* He looks over at Charlice. Smiles. *This is where I want to be.*

Charlice looks over at William and smiles back. She thinks, *Damn he got me with the great dick on the kitchen floor. Why do men think good spontaneous sex solves everything? I'm not going down this married man path again.*

She sits up on the floor, puts her pants back on and says, "Okay! Let's eat before my chicken and shrimp Alfredo overcooks. You set the table while I go wash up. Then we can talk and eat."

William is still laying on the floor confused. "Wait…We still need to talk?"

Charlice laughs as she goes upstairs.

"In situations of captivity the perpetrator becomes the most powerful person in the life of the victim, and the psychology of the victim is shaped by the actions and beliefs of the perpetrator."

— Judith Lewis Herman, Trauma and Recovery: The Aftermath of Violence - From Domestic Abuse to Political Terror

Chapter V: The Psychological Laceration

The Open Wound

"Tonight is THE Night. The All Challenges Mastered A Taste of Ivory Soiree: All White Gala at The Winston Hotel. Hosted by yours truly Peaches CEO of A Taste of Peaches. This event is the annual event to raise money for the nonprofit organization, All Challenges Mastered, which is a local nonprofit organization that focuses on breaking down the challenges that our young people face. And you know how we party in DC…good food, Mambo sauce and of course GO-GO music. If y'all miss this event, I don't know what to tell you. You gon' be mad at yourself.

Tickets, if any are still available, can be purchased on Eventbrite. If you just want to donate to this worthy cause, go to their website. All proceeds go to the organization. I hope to see you tonight in your sexiest white ensembles." Peaches stops her recording. Then posts the video on all of her social media platforms. "Now that should get the rest of those tickets sold."

Peaches is the best event planner in the DMV. Even though her services are very expensive, she is worth it. If anyone wanted a party, they would call Peaches and her

Taste of Peaches Team.

Peaches also planned trips around the world with the rich and famous. Because she works for the DC government, she knows everyone. She works in the Mayor's Office, the Community Affairs Division. That is where she makes most of her connections.

Not only does she work for the mayor, she is having a secret love affair with him. Mayor Kent Anderson, a DC native and graduate of the University of DC, is married to Latasha Wilson- Anderson. Latasha is a Howard University Alumni from Brooklyn, New York.

Peaches loves the connections that she has made because of the mayor. Only one person knows about this secret love affair...Karen. Peaches shares one of her deepest secrets with Karen. Peaches entrusted Karen with her secret because she had no choice. Karen walked in on Kent and Peaches kissing and dry humping on Peaches' beautiful white sofa one day. So Peaches had to tell her about the affair and swore her to secrecy. Peaches knows her secret is safe with Karen because Karen enjoys the clout and the status that she gains by being in Peaches' circle.

"Oh shoot." Peaches shouts out. "I'm about to be late for my appointment at Majestic." Majestic is a suite located in DC. Peaches loves that she can go into a less semi private location and have all of her beauty services taken care of. Because this was a special occasion, that is exactly what she was about to do. This was HER event and she had to be the Baddest Bit** at the party.

Peaches is hype. She grabs her cell phone, her wallet, her Gucci shades and the fob to her black Mercedes E Class Cabriolet convertible and heads out the door and down the hallway to the elevator that leads to the underground parking garage.

On the way to the garage, her phone rings. Peaches looks down at the phone; smiles. Seductively she answers, "Hello Mr. Mayor. How can I serve you today?"

"Ooh! Do you think I will get a taste of Peaches after this gala tonight? You know how I just love my Peaches." A deep male voice says on the other end of the phone.

"Mr. Mayor, you know you can ALWAYS have a taste. Make sure you clear it with your wife first. I would hate for her to run up on something that she ain't prepared to see." Peaches throws that in to get his reaction.

He laughs, "I am not worried about Mrs. Mayor. I am the mayor. I need to check on my city before I return home. I need to make sure the bed in the suite that I reserved is firm enough for me to serve my Peaches on. As the mayor, I have duties and responsibilities to my constituents. Plus, we need to have a debriefing about this event. Do you understand Miss Peaches?"

"Oh I understand Mr. Mayor. Hopefully, you can focus on your wife at the gala once you see me tonight. But I will DEFINITELY be ready for my debriefing afterwards sir."

"Sounds like a meeting. I will have one of my bodyguards bring you the key card to the room. Once he brings you the card, I will be in the room in about two hours. Don't keep me waiting too long. I'm going to be real hungry." Kent hangs up the phone.

Peaches shakes her head. She loves having sex with Kent. Does she love him…Nah! But more than anything she loves the connections that he brings her. Their relationship is mutually beneficial. She provides him with the events where he can bond with the community so that he can get more votes and she brings the people with the money to these events.

The great sex is a bonus. Peaches could care less about his wife. Kent's infidelity is his wife's problem. When it ends between them, it ends. They will both move on. But until then, she is going to meet him after the gala for great sex in a gorgeous suite in a prestigious hotel. The perfect way to end the evening.

In her car, she decides to call Karen. "Hey Karen! Are you ready for tonight?"

"Hey girl! Not yet. I am running around now. I am on my way to Lou's salon so she can do my hair and Sam can do my makeup. My stylist is bringing my outfit to the house later. Then I will be on my way. The question is are YOU ready for tonight?"

"YES!" Peaches screams. "I am heading to Majestic now to

get my hair done. I have reserved a room at the hotel for me to get dressed and to get my face beat. One of my team members is stopping by my penthouse to pick up everything that I need. You are welcome to come get ready with me and Khrystina if you like."

"I will probably come up. I have to check in with William first to see what time he is getting the kids. We went to the circus the other day. I will have to tell you all about that. Today is not the day. But girl, I have a story for you." Karen says.

"Yes, your story has to wait. Because after tonight, I am going to have a story for you. Kent got a room for him and me in the hotel. He is being real bold, meeting his mistress in the same hotel where his wife is attending a gala." Peaches switches to a serious tone, "As for you, I told you William loves you. He ain't going nowhere. Give him his space. He will be back. Watch. Mark my words."

Karen, sounding reassured, "Okay! I hear you, friend." Karen trusts Peaches and knows that she would never tell her anything that does not make sense.

"That's right. Trust your big sister friend. I am at Majestic. I will see you tonight." Peaches blows Karen a kiss and ends the call.

Karen pulls up to *Salon A'dore*. She checks her makeup in the mirror and gets out of her Range Rover. She walks into the salon and announces her presence. "Hello everyone! I have arrived. I am practicing for my grand entrance at The Taste of Ivory Soiree: All White." This was her way of letting everyone know that she was attending THE social event of the year.

Karen walks past the receptionist, raises her hand to speak and heads over to Lou's chair. "Hey Lou! Make me more beautiful than I already am so my husband will want me even more. Then we can go home and make baby number three tonight."

Lou sucks her teeth, as she pauses styling her current clients hair just to look at Karen. "Hey Karen! Have a seat. I will be with you momentarily." Lou is unbothered by Karen's announcement.

Sam is working on a client at his station. He ignores Karen as well. Everyone ignores Karen.

Karen has no clue that everyone is ignoring her. She flops down in Lou's chair, as if she is exhausted. Then looks in the mirror and begins to prepare her hair for styling. She is so anxious for someone to ask her a question about tonight. "Oh my goodness! Lou, what are we going to do for my hair this evening? My hair has to be perfect for the gala tonight. Everyone who is anybody in DC is going to be there. Is anyone else going or just me?"

Sam has had enough, he stops styling his client, "Look Kar'n don't nobody up in here care about your little fake bougie event."

Karen is startled and stone faced by Sam's rant.

"You see Kar'n all of us up in here are REAL MoFo's. We ain't got no time to be trying to impress people that don't give a damn about us. Half y'all up in there will have spent money on outfits, makeup, nails and cars for just this one night. Some of y'all got the tags to your clothes taped up under your clothes so you can return them the next day. Some of y'all went into debt and spent money that you really didn't have for this one night. Some of y'all need to worry 'bout yo' kids and some of y'all need to worry about other things such as who is sleeping wit' your man instead of worrying about who you impressed at a damn party. Get the fuck outta here Kar'n." Sam pops his tongue against his teeth and goes back to styling his client who has put her face into her magazine to hide the expression on her face.

The salon is silent. Lou looks down. Everyone is looking down or away except Karen. Karen is looking at Sam.

Karen in shock utters, "Well where do I fit in with your assessment of gala participants, Sam?"

Everyone looks up in anticipation of Sam's answer.

Sam stops working again, looks at Karen, "Only you and your God can answer that one KaREN." He keeps working.

The rest of Karen's time in the salon is spent in silence.

While Lou does her hair, Karen is fairly silent. Lou is asking her questions about William, the kids, her other events but Karen keeps giving her short answers. *This is not like Karen. Sam must have hurt her feelings.* Lou thinks.

Once Lou is finished, Karen goes into the makeup room with Sam, the self-declared, Makeup Guru. He is one of the best in the DMV though. While Sam does Karen's makeup. He tries to talk to her but she keeps giving him short answers. "Look KaREN! I am sorry if I offended you when I was talking about your little soiree." He pops his tongue on the roof of his mouth. "You already know that I give everyone a hard time. This is who I am." *Sam still remembered how Karen talked to him a few months back, but money is money. And he is not going to turn it away.*

"Oh Sam, it's okay. I am not upset. I understand that some people are upset that they can't afford to attend tonight's All White Soiree. It's okay." She then starts to whisper. "I know people are very jealous of me and my lavish lifestyle. I try to be empathetic to the less fortunate."

Sam pauses for a second trying to process what Karen just said. He thinks *Is this crazy bitch serious?* Sam burst out laughing, "Kar'n you can NOT be serious. Ain't nobody here jealous of you or your life? While you running around here talking to imaginary people, you need to talk to Jesus so he can get your crazy ass straight."

Karen laughs as she admires herself in the mirror.

As Sam finishes up, William walks in to pay for Karen's

services. "Hey everyone! How is everyone doing today?"

"Hey William!" Lou says. Karen is in the back room. Sam is finishing up her face."

William pays the receptionist and heads to the back room. He sees Karen. "Wow! You look amazing Karen. Sam, you did a wonderful job. I guess that's why they call you the Makeup Guru."

"And you know it." Sam looks William up and down.

"Why aren't you going to the gala, Mr. Lime?" Lou asks, as she walks in the room.

William says, "Humph! I'm good. Maybe in my younger days I would have attended but now the only person/people that I need to impress are my children by being a stand up dad; someone they can look up to."

"I know that's right." Sam adds looking at Karen.

"Karen, I am going to head out and go pick up the kids from school and take them to my house."

"What? You aren't coming to the house to see me off and see me in my gorgeous white outfit?"

"I am sorry. I made plans for the kids and I immediately after school. I already paid for your services today. I will see you Sunday when I drop the kids off." William heads towards the door.

"Aww!" Karen sounds disappointed. "Well I will send you plenty of pictures so you can see me in my sexy white outfit."

"Oh okay! Have fun Karen!" William scurries out the door.

Karen calls after him to ask for a kiss but she is too late. She sees him standing in front of the shop. He is talking to Charlice.

Karen watches as William grabs Charlice's hand and she slides it away smiling. *What is really going on between them?* She thinks.

As William heads to his car, Charlice walks in and sits in Lou's chair.

Sam removes the cape from Karen and Karen deliberately sashays her way back to Lou's station.

"Ooh! This about to be good." Sam had seen the little flirty banter between Charlice and William too.

Karen walks over to Lou. "Lou, thank you so much for doing my hair for the gala. It is perfect, as usual. I am going to be the Belle of the Gala. Oh, hello Charpiece! It is so nice to see you again. Did you find a house for William and I yet?"

"Hello, Mrs. Lime. It is nice to see you again as well. Remember I am your husband's realtor. You need to ask him, not me. You look amazing. I'm sure you are going to have a wonderful time tonight at the All White Gala."

Karen stands there hitting her left fist on her left thigh. "Yes, everyone who's anyone is going to be there. So I guess you all will be home. I will bring plenty of pictures when I come back next week. Toodles!" Karen rushes out the door.

"Goodbye Mrs. Lime! I will be sure to tell your husband you said hey when I am riding him tonight." Charlice smirks.

Lou laughs, "You are wrong girl! Just mean and wrong."

"She called me Charpiece. She knows my name. Now come on and do my hair so Karen's man can sweat it out later." Lou can only shake her head at the Bermuda Triangle.

"So you and William are good now after the circus incident?" Lou asks.

"Yes we are great. I still haven't met the kids. I am meeting them tonight so the next time Karen comes in here she is going to have a lot of questions and she is going to have a lot to say about me."

Sam and Sandy come into the room.

"Mind you." Lou says, "Sam and Sandy, as my witnesses, she is crazy so be careful. I don't know what she is capable of when she finds out her beloved William has another woman."

***

Even though The Taste of Ivory Soiree started at eight o'clock pm, Peaches made her grand entrance at 9 o'clock pm.

She and the DJ had arranged that at 8:55 p.m. he would play music that made people clear the dance floor. Then at 9 o'clock he would play Go-Go music and announce her entrance.

At 8:55, Peaches waited patiently behind the doors to the ballroom. Through a small space between the doors, she could see the sea of all the beautiful bougie elite of the DMV dressed in all white. It was amazing. She had pulled it off.

The clock strikes 9 o'clock and the DJ turns on the Go-Go and announces the host Peaches. Peaches comes out through the double doors Beatin' her Feet like the DC native that she is. The crowd goes wild as they look on and hype Peaches up.

The DJ turns the music down and passes the microphone to Peaches. Peaches thanks everyone for coming to The Taste of Ivory Soiree: All White Gala. She thanks the mayor, her friends and all of the supporters for attending the fundraiser. She ends her speech with "Now everyone enjoy the good food and the music. And let's just all have a good time."

She works her way through the crowd and over to her VIP

table where Karen is sitting along with her friend Khrystina and some more people.

"Great speech Peaches. You look amazing." Says Khrystina as she gives Peaches a hug.

Karen chimes in, "Yes you look gorgeous. This party is the bomb. Everybody who is anybody in DC is here."

"Yes! I told you. Thank you both for being here and supporting me. I appreciate you both. Now come on friends. Let's go out here and dance. Let's go out here and show these men what they are missing." Peaches says as she pulls her friends to the dance floor.

The three women are having a good time on the dance floor. The women are interrupted several times by men at the party who want to dance with them. Peaches encourages her friends to dance. "It's just a dance. It's not like you're cheating on your husbands."

A man dressed in a black suit walks over to Peaches. Whispers in her ear and discreetly places a key card in her hand. Peaches slips the card into one of the pockets of the white dress that she is wearing.

On the other side of the ballroom, there seems to be a commotion. Peaches quickly stops dancing to investigate the noise.

In a corner by the restrooms, a man and woman are arguing.

A tall muscular man wearing all white accented with gold jewelry is yelling at a woman, "You told me that you had to work late and that's why you couldn't pick up the kids. You didn't tell me that you were hoeing around DC."

The woman looks surprised by the man as she is trying to go into the restroom. She is about to respond but then another man walks over to the pair. He stands between them and calmly says, "Gerald this is not the time or place to discuss this. You and Jaime can discuss this later. I suggest that you go back with your friends and enjoy the party."

Gerald pushes the man back. Then yells, "I told you once before mind your own business. You ought to thank me for allowing you to rent my wife. I haven't sold her yet, and until I do, you need to fall back and let me handle my own family affairs."

The boyfriend holds his arms up, surrendering to the push. "I understand what you are saying but this is not the place right now to discuss family business and I'm not going to allow you to talk crazy to my woman." Then he pulls the woman close to him.

The angry husband pulls back and hits the boyfriend. That is when the real fight starts.

Peaches signals the DJ to stop the music and direct security to the area near the restrooms. The party goers are scattering. Some walk towards the fight, others, are grabbing their possessions to leave. The mayor is in an opposite corner being protected by his security officers.

The husband, Gerald, is beating the boyfriend pretty badly. The estranged wife Jaime is trying to pull her husband off of her boyfriend but her husband's friends are holding her back.

Security breaks up the fight. The fighters' beautiful white attire is splattered and soaked with blood.

The husband is still talking, "This ain't over punk. I will see you outside. You too, Jaime."

The boyfriend, being held by security, says, "Yeah outside."

Jaime grabs her and Maurice's things. She is so upset that she is shaking.

Peaches walks over to her; gives her a hug. "Are you okay? Do you need anything dear?'

Jaime is crying, "I am so sorry Peaches for the drama at your party. Maurice and I will be fine."

"Good! Good! Security is going to walk you two to the door." Peaches empathetically shows Jaime and Maurice to the door. *Try to ruin my party. They need to go.*

Peaches signals to the DJ to crank the music back up. The party must go on despite the fact that some people had left already.

As Jaime and Maurice head towards the door. Maurice *sees Gerald standing out front with his boys. Gerald is warming up getting ready for a fight. I am tired of fighting with this man. His wife and I have been together for about a year now. He has already beaten me up three times. Now he has his friends with him. Eventually, he is going to kill me or Jaime.*

Jaime hands their ticket to the valet to bring their car around. "Once the car pulls up, we can just jump in and go home. Forget him. We can deal with him later."

Maurice does not hear her. He is in deep thought. *If I can just get to my trunk, I can end all of this.*

Peaches notices that Jaime left her phone on the table. She hands the phone to Karen. "Can you please take this out to the young lady who was just involved in that fight?"

"Sure no problem. Anything for you friend." Karen heads out to the lobby. The couple is no longer in the lobby.

As she is walking towards the door to the hotel entrance, she notices that a valet is opening the car door for Jaime. So she starts running towards the car. Yelling, "Ma'am, your phone. You forgot your…"

All of a sudden, Karen hears two men arguing. Karen cannot make out what is being said. People are shouting.

All Karen stops running and starts slowly walking as she hears: Leave my wife alone…Back up…Imma beat yo' ass

96

again…Get him…I warned you… Oh shit! GUN…I'm not afraid of you…Duck!…Do it…Go ahead…Do it…

"Pull the trigger!" Someone yells.

POW! POW! POW! POW! POW! POW! POW! POW!

"NOOOOO!!!"

Karen pauses at the sound of gunshots.

She drops the phone and slaps both hands over her ears.

Karen is frozen as she starts to scream in sheer terror.

She runs over to a corner outside the entrance of the hotel, and balls her body up into a fetal position still screaming, shaking, and sweating.

Peaches comes running out of the ballroom to find out exactly what is going on outside of her party. She sees people running and covering their heads; people are laying on the ground. As she gets closer to the chaos. As she gets closer, she can hear a sound of a woman screaming. When she looks towards the sound, she finds her friend balled up in the corner screaming at the top of her lungs.

"DADDDDDDAYYY! DADDDDAYYYYY! DADDDAYYYYY!"

"Stronger than lover's love is lover's hate. Incurable, in each, the wounds they make."— Euripides, Medea

Chapter VI: The Lifeless Impetus

The Reason for Motive

As Karen lay balled up in the corner screaming, crying, shaking and kicking, she recalls the details of the most tragic day of her life. The shooting at the Ivory Soiree triggers something in Karen. Something deep inside her that she had been suppressing. And it all started with Lordess.

***

Lordess is a beautiful young Afro-Latina Honduran woman who lives in Texas. She is what the streets call a Cub, a Come Up Bunny; a woman who looks for the men with the money.

Lordess had learned how to be a Cub when she was very young. She learned this way of life from some of the older, more experienced Cubs that she grew up around. They would say, "Lordess don't ever date a broke man. If a man can't take care of you, he ain't worth having. Don't ever give the milk away for free." Lordess listened to and studied and followed the teachings of her mentors. Eventually she developed her own style and became a master at the art of being a Cub.

As a Cub master, Lordess, who was still in high school, always had several men giving her money and buying her gifts.

Lordess was a beautiful darker skinned Afro Latina. People would often mistake her for someone from the islands because of her exotic features.

When one man would ask her for an exclusive relationship or for sex, she would move on to the next man or she would just get rid of the man.

At one point, Lordess was getting tired of the older dudes so she started focusing her attention on younger guys. Younger guys with potential. One particular guy; a new guy named Kevin. Kevin, whose parents are of Nigerian descent, is a basketball and track star at her high school. All the college scouts are looking at him. To Lordess, college scouts meant the NBA and everyone knows the NBA means money.

There was just one thing keeping them from being together. Kevin had a girlfriend named Sophia, a quiet, studious, white Brazilian girl who loved Kevin and was loved by Kevin. LOVE? This did not stop Lordess from pursuing Kevin though.

Using most of her Cub skills, Lordess managed to seduce and get him into bed. Then she made sure that Sophia found out about her and Kevin. She showed Sophia some of the messages that she and Kevin had exchanged. She even showed Sophia pictures of them together.

Because he loves Sophia, Kevin admits to cheating with Lordess. He apologizes to Sophia and they decide to work on their relationship. He vows to never see Lordess again.

When Kevin explains to Lordess that he and Sophia are going to stay together, Lordess lies and tells him that she is pregnant. Even though he loves Sophia, Kevin breaks up with Sophia. Because of his family values, he feels that he must marry Lordess and be a father to his child.

Sophia understands but then explains to him that she is pregnant too. Lordess convinces him that Sophia is lying. Kevin believes Lordess so they end up getting married because Lordess didn't want Sophia to have him.

Because of his moral obligation to family, Kevin turned down the college scholarship offers so that he could stay home and take care of his wife and child.

Lordess is furious because now her main meal ticket is gone and she had given up all of her other men so she could be with Kevin, the NBA player.

Since she faked her pregnancy, she has to come up with a lie so she tells Kevin that all of the stress with Sophia and him not going to college has caused her to lose the baby. Although Kevin is upset about the loss of his child, he loves Lordess and does everything he can to make her happy.

He works two jobs to make sure that he takes care of all of the needs of his wife. He doesn't want her to work. He just wants her to stay home and take care of the home.

Eventually, Lordess does get pregnant. They have a beautiful baby girl that they name Karen Adanna.

Karen means pure and Adanna is Nigerian for father's daughter. Kevin was so in love with his daughter. When he first saw his little girl, Karen, Kevin vowed to give her the world and to always protect her.

After about two years of marriage, Kevin and Lordess are settled into a decent life. They are one little happy family… until that one day.

There is a light knock on their door.

Kevin answers the door. "Sophia? What a pleasant surprise." He reaches out to hug her. He hugs her tightly.

Lordess, who is in the kitchen with Karen, hears him say Sophia. *What does she want now?* She grabs her baby and heads towards the door.

When Lordess gets to the door, with Karen on her hip, she sees Kevin hugging Sophia, who is holding a small boy.

Kevin stops hugging her when he hears Lordess coming from the kitchen.

"Look who it is." Kevin says to Lordess.

Lordess just stands there looking at him not making eye contact with Sophia or her baby.

Kevin turns back around to Sophia. "Who is this handsome young fellow?" Kevin asks, playing with the leg of the small child who is clutched tightly to Sophia's hip but laughing at Kevin who apparently touched his ticklish spot.

"Kevin," Sophia pauses and looks over at Lordess then looks back at Kevin, "This is your son, Kevin. We call him KJ. I felt that it was time that you two met."

Before Kevin can utter a word, Lordess has something to say, "Whose son? You are kidding me Sophia. You just walk in here and tell my husband that you have his baby. We ain't seen you in years."

"I know it has been a long time but Lordess if you recall, I told Kevin that I was pregnant. For some reason, he thought that I was lying. Kevin was my first and only at the time. KJ is his son. You do the math."

"I got some math for you Sophia." Lordess gets closer to Sophia "One plus one plus one equals three. This is Karen. Karen is our daughter. My daughter with Kevin. This is our family. You need to leave our home. NOW!"

"I will go." Sophia utters. "Kevin, KJ and I will see you in court."

"No Sophia! Don't go." Kevin walks towards her. "I would like to spend some time with my son. There is no need for the courts to get involved. I know KJ is my son. I was a young fool. I should have listened to my heart. I knew you were pregnant. I saw you."

"What? You believe her?" Lordess is furious.

"Yes! Yes, I do Lordess. Sophia never lied to me when we were together. I don't know what happened. But I do know this is my son and I want to be part of his life. Sophia, please have a seat so you and I can work out some arrangements for our son."

Lordess takes Karen back in the kitchen. She is furious. Her life is falling apart. Lordess knows that she has lost control of Kevin. *I need to go back to my old ways. I got so wrapped up in this family thing. I am off my game a little bit.*

Over the next few weeks, Kevin starts to spend more time with KJ and Sophia. He spends less time with Lordess and Karen. When he is home, he tries to avoid Lordess. He spends most of his time with Karen.

Lordess finally decides that she has had enough of his disrespect so she decides to pull Kevin up on his behavior. "Kevin, what the hell is going on with you?"

"Nothing Lordess. What do you mean?"

"What do I mean? Are you serious? You barely come home anymore. When I call you, you don't answer me. Tell me what is going on so that I can be prepared."

"Prepared?" Kevin asks.

"Yes! Prepared. You think I'm going to let some man disrespect me and I am going to sit here and watch him disrespect me. Humph! I thought you knew me better than that." Lordess rolls her eyes.

"It's not that Lordess. It's just that… It's just that…"

"It's just that what? Spit it out. Say what you have to say."

"Lordess, I loved Sophia a few years ago. I was her first love. She was such a good girl. She was telling the truth about being pregnant and I accused her of lying. I missed two years of my son's life that I cannot get back."

"Oh so now you are trying to get those two years back by throwing me and your daughter away? You cannot get that time back nor can you get back the time that you are missing with me and Karen. These are important years for her. These are important years for your marriage. You are supposed to be taking care of home. Instead you are out trying to go back in time. Let it go!"

"But Lordess, I walked away from Sophia as well. I accused her of being a liar. She is one of the sweetest women that I have ever met. How could I have done that to her?"

"Kevin, you sound like you still have feelings for her…." Lordess asks.

Kevin is silent. Kevin looks down.

"KEVIN, do you have something to tell me? Kevin, are you in love with her? KEVIN, DO…YOU…LOVE…HER?"

Kevin looks at Lordess confusedly, "I don't know. I just don't know."

"What do you mean? Did you have sex with her?"

Kevin starts crying, "Lordess, I am sorry. I am so sorry." He tries to grab Lordess' hand to pull her close to him. He needed a hug from her.

Lordess pulls away angry, "So you did. You had sex with her. I can't believe you. I can't believe you would do this to us. GET OUT!"

Kevin is down on his knees begging, pleading, crying, "Lordess, please, please, please forgive me. Look at me. I am begging you. I did not plan for it to happen. I felt guilty. I felt bad. I don't know why I did it. I love you, Lordess. I love our Karen, I love our family."

"Do you really love us, Kevin? Do you REALLY love us Kevin?" Lordess asks angrily but without tears.

"Yes Lordess! I promise I will make this right." Kevin says still on his knees.

"Then I need you to do one thing for me."

"Anything, Lordess. What is it?" Kevin wipes his tears.

"I need you to leave Sophia and her bastard baby alone.

Promise me that you will never see them again."

Kevin stands up. "So you want me to abandon my son and the mother of my child again?"

"Yes Kevin," Lordess declares sinisterly, "or I am leaving and taking Karen with me. You choose." Then she folds her arms and sits down on the sofa.

"As you wish, Lordess." Kevin was distraught. "I choose my wife and my daughter."

At that moment, two things happened. One, Kevin realizes how evil Lordess is; he realizes that he was tricked into this marriage. He was manipulated by Lordess. Two, Lordess realizes that she has been betrayed by Kevin. She will not be betrayed again. She realizes that it is time for the old Lordess to come back. Yes, she loves Kevin, but she has a lifestyle that she needs to maintain and Kevin doesn't make enough for her to live that lifestyle. *Love, forget that. I now have a daughter who needs to be schooled on the ways of a Cub. Yes, I think it is time.*

***

Lordess never got past the betrayal that she felt from Kevin not to mention the fact that Kevin continued to sneak over to see Sophia and their son. Since Kevin wanted to step outside the marriage, Lordess continued to see men outside of their marriage. Eventually, Lordess started seeing a man named Oscar. The streets named called him "O".

Oscar was a young man from El Salvador who was more than happy to take care of Lordess. Even though he was a few years younger than Lordess, he loved how mature she was. A man like him needed an experienced woman. Oscar was well known in the streets of Houston, Texas. He did not have a regular nine to five job. He had a job that paid in cash. Lots of cash.

Oscar was involved in the distribution of street pharmaceuticals and all of the other illegal activities that came along with it. He wasn't a corner boy but he managed several corners and multiple businesses in his neighborhood. Everyone knew Oscar and everyone knew that he was not someone whose bad side you wanted to be on.

Lordess had met Oscar years ago but she was committed to her marriage at the time. Lordess just kept in touch with him when she needed a couple of dollars here and there. But now that Kevin had betrayed her, she made Oscar her main man on the side.

Everyone in the streets knew that Lordess was Oscar's woman. Everyone except Kevin. Kevin had heard talk about Lordess and some guy but he ignored them because he loved Lordess. He noticed all of the designer handbags, clothes, and shoes that she was wearing. He noticed all the designer clothing that Karen was wearing. He knew that he couldn't afford them. However, Lordess was his wife and he believed in upholding his wedding vows.

Plus, she was still there with him so she must believe in their vows as well.

But more than anything, he loved his baby girl, Karen. Karen was now a beautiful eight-year-old girl whose face lit up every time she saw him. When he looked at Karen, it was like looking at himself. His son, KJ, resembled Sophia. But Karen was all him. She has his rich dark complexion, his large puppy dog brown eyes, his long curly eyelashes and she was clearly going to be tall like him with just a little thickness to her.

Karen loved her dad so much. Her dad bought her whatever she wanted. He gave her everything that she needed. For Karen life was perfect until it wasn't anymore.

Oscar was very controlling and abusive to Lordess. One day while Lordess and Oscar were laying in his bed Oscar tells Lordess, "You need to leave that weak ass husband of yours and come live with me.

"I cannot do that. I have to think of my daughter. She loves her dad. I would never separate them." Lordess contests.

"Huh? You can't leave? I'm not understanding you." Oscar is now sitting up getting angry with Lordess' defiance. "Just leave your daughter with him. You can have more kids can't you?"

Now Lordess sits up, "Yes I can have more kids but I'm not leaving my daughter. I could never do that to her. Kevin has been a great father to her.

Their bond is unbreakable."

Oscar thinks for a moment. Gets up and starts to get dressed. "Unbreakable huh?" He shakes his head like yeah.

"Unbreakable." Lordess whispers.

"Bet! I got you. I will take care of it." Oscar grabs his keys and bolts towards the door.

"Oscar, what are you going to do?" Lordess yells worriedly.

He turns around quickly, furiously. Points his finger towards her and replies, "Don't ask me no damn questions. I got this." He pats his gun in the holster on his right hip. Nods and walks back towards the door.

Lordess is worried for Kevin but she is afraid to warn him. If she tells him, then she has to admit to the affair. If she admits to the affair, she may lose her daughter.

Lordess is afraid of Oscar. She knows his temper. *How did I get myself into this? What do I tell Kevin?* Lordess grabs her phone and calls Kevin.

"Hey Babe! How are you?" Kevin asks, surprised to hear from his wife in the middle of the day.

"Hey Dear! Are you at work or are you out to lunch somewhere? If you haven't had lunch, I thought that perhaps you and I could meet for lunch today. You know…Like we used to do."

Lordess was trying to figure out exactly where he was so that she could make sure she was around him. She figured that if she was with Kevin, Oscar would not do anything crazy.

"Oh that would have been nice." Kevin was confused by Lordess' niceness. *I wonder what she really wants.* "Remember I am leaving early today so that I can pick Karen up from school and take her to the circus so I won't be having lunch today."

"Oh that is right. I forgot." Lordess is relieved because she just knows that Oscar would never harm Kevin in front of Karen. *He is safe for now. I will talk to Oscar later and we can figure this out.* "Okay! Well you and Karen enjoy your time together. I will see you when you get home. I love you!"

Kevin was taken aback, "I…I love you too, Lordess." *She hasn't told me that she loves me in years. I hope she isn't sick. Maybe she has decided to forgive me for my slip ups with Sophia. Maybe she has decided to accept KJ into our family. Maybe she has decided to end her affair and commit herself to our marriage. Who knows?*

At 3:00, Kevin arrives at Karen's school to pick her up. He waits on the sidewalk in front of the building with all of the other moms and dads. He starts a conversation with another dad about their daughters and about the special bond between a father and his daughter.

To celebrate attending the circus, Kevin has bought a gift for Karen. It is a pink long-handled mirror with a little brown girl wearing a tutu, riding a unicycle. Kevin always wants his daughter to remember how beautiful she is and how much she is loved by him so on special occasions like this he buys her special gifts to commemorate special days. Today he is more excited than she is. He finally gets to spend a daddy-daughter day with Karen.

The dismissal bell rings and the kids start fluttering out of the building. Some are running. Some are playing with their friends. Some are just walking around looking for their parents. But the one thing that all share is their pure innocence. *They all look so innocent walking out of the building.* Kevin thought as he patiently waited for his daughter to come out of the building.

As little innocent Karen came out of the building, she was looking around for her dad. She knew he was coming. She was so excited. She got to spend time with her dad. She was about to spend a daddy/daughter day with her most favorite person in the whole entire world. The anticipation of just seeing him was building up inside of her as she was looking around for him.

AH HA! Found him! Karen's heart starts pounding faster as she sees her dad with a gift bag in his hand. *But what is Mommy's friend "O" doing with Daddy? Is "O" coming with us? Where is Mommy?* Her pounding heart slows down.

112

Kevin notices that Karen's smile is turning into confusion. He looks to his left and sees a man. (*A dad?*) Standing next to him. He looks at him and smiles. The dad just looks at him. Kevin squats down and opens his arms to receive a hug from Karen.

Karen smiles and begins walking towards her dad's open arms.

"O" is still standing there. Looking down at Kevin. Then looking at Karen. Legs spread slightly apart. Arms folded in front of him. Right hand clenching the left hand. No smile. Silent. Watching. Waiting.

All around the school grounds kids are scurrying to buses, to cars, to their parents, to their safe spaces. All the hustle and bustle of kids trying to make it to their safe spaces, including Karen.

Karen reaches out to her dad. Her safe place. She grabs his right hand. Just as Kevin is about to pull Karen into his arms someone steps in between them. The masked man pushes Kevin. Kevin falls back on the ground. Karen and Kevin's hands separate. The masked man bends down, his beady eyes meet Karen's big brown eyes; he looks at Karen. Then whispers, "Unbreakable huh? Watch this little girl."

The masked man pulls out a big black gun. Points it at Kevin who is laying on the ground with his hands up in the don't shoot position. He looks over at frightened innocent

Karen. The masked man staring at Karen, "Humph! Remember you did this. This was all your fault baby girl."

The masked man cocks the gun back, "Lordess wants out." Then he shoots Kevin eight times. Seven shots in the body and the eighth one right between Kevin's eyes.

Children, parents, teachers are running frantically. Terrified. Screaming. Crying…Karen is frozen. She glares at the masked man, who is now running away.

As he is running, he is yelling, "Eight shots for you Lil' Mama. Eight shots for every year of your life. Eight shots for your unbreakable bond. No more bond…"

Just then a black car with dark tinted windows quickly pulls up to the curve. The masked man hops in the front passenger seat of the car. The passenger side window comes down slowly. Karen and the masked man lock eyes. The man reaches his hand out the window to point his imaginary gun as if he is shooting her. He burst out laughing and the car sped away.

Karen looks over at Kevin who is laying in a pool of blood on the sidewalk of her school. The blood is flowing down the sidewalk like spilled milk. Blood is oozing and squirting from various holes in his body. Blood is trickling out the right side of his mouth. The bullet between his eyes looks like a tiny spot of dirt on his forehead. He is looking over at Karen. He is wiggling his fingers as if he wants her to come to him.

When Kevin moves his fingers, she is no longer frozen. Karen runs over to her dad, lays down beside him and puts her head on his shoulder. "Daddy, please don't leave me. Daddy please." She begs. "I love you." Tears are running down her face.

With the last bit of energy that he can muster up, Kevin clutches Karen's hand which is pressed up against his hand. Startled by his sudden movement, Karen looks up into his eyes hoping that he is about to get up and hoping that everything will be alright.

But it's not. Kevin looks into Karen's eyes; smiles. Then closes his eyes.

"DADDDDDDAYYY! DADDDDAYYYYY! DADDDAYYYYY!" Karen screams not noticing her clothes, face, shoes and book bag are soaked in the blood of her father.

She doesn't even notice the blaring sirens of the police cars, the ambulances or the fire trucks.

She only notices something as she is being pulled away from her dad and laid on the ground to be examined by the paramedics. Karen lay kicking and screaming for Kevin but her dad is not answering. She sees him. He is just lying there on the sidewalk. *Why aren't they helping him?*

"HELP MY DADDY!" Karen screams in anger. "Help him! Please." She pleads.

Karen tries to run over to Kevin but she is held down. Then strapped to a gurney; whisked into an ambulance.

As the ambulance drives off, Karen looks out the ambulance window. She can see the front of her school. The lawn is littered with police, cameras, news reporters and just people coming to look. Then she sees the spot where her dad lay. A white sheet is covering where her dad lies. Next to the white sheet is a pink gift bag with the blood of her father seeping through the bottom of it.

Karen lay on the gurney thinking. She will never forget those beady eyes. *Unbreakable? What does that mean? Why? Why? Why?* Karen starts snapping her head back on the gurney and hitting her fist on her left thigh, the hand that her father last touched. "Why? Why? Why?" She asks as she attempts to kick, scream and yell. She stops exhausted and frustrated.

"No motive is pure. No one is good or bad-but a hearty mix of both. And sometimes life actually gives to you by taking away."— Carrie Fisher, Wishful Drinking

116

Chapter VII: *The Impressive Consideration*

Deep Thoughts

Karen Lime slowly opens her eyes. Then closes them. She feels groggy. *I need to get up*. She thinks. But someone gently pushes her back. She attempts to open her eyes but her eyelids feel so heavy.

A familiar calming deep voice whispers in her ear, "Everything is okay Karen. You are safe. Lay back down. We are here."

"We?" Karen says, confused and tries to get up again but she can't move. Her wrists are restrained by something. All she can do is wiggle her fingers and rotate her wrists. "Where..." She utters. But she can barely speak. She is too tired.

"You are in the hospital." Another familiar calm, woman's voice speaks.

Feeling safe, Karen lays her head back down and drifts off to sleep again.

When Karen wakes up, she is wide awake. Her eyes are wide open and she can move her wrists freely.

117

She looks around the sterile hospital room. All four walls are a crisp white. On one of the walls, there is a large window covered with thick black bars. There is nothing else in the room except Peaches. Peaches is standing by the closed door. Her back is to Karen and she is talking on the phone. There is nothing else in the room. No television. No chair. No closet. No bathroom. Just her and the four white walls. "Peaches, where am I?" She tries to speak but her mouth is extremely dry so it is difficult for her to say anything.

Peaches turns around when she hears a noise. "Karen," She says excitedly. "You are awake. Finally, girl. You scared me. You scared all of us." She gives Karen a big hug.

"Us?" Karen is confused. "Peaches, what happened? Where am I? Where are the kids? Where is William...WILLIAM? WILLIAM?" Karen starts to get agitated.

"Calm down dear. You are okay. You are in the hospital." Peaches anxiously presses the call button for a nurse or a doctor. *Somebody needs to come get her. I don't know how to handle crazy people.*

William comes busting through the door. "Karen, I am right here." He pushes Peaches away so that Karen can see him. "What is wrong?" He offers her a side hug.

"Will, what is going on? Why am I here? What happened?" She pulls him closer and lays her head on his chest and begins to sob. She is sobbing because she remembers the

118

last time she was in a hospital room like this. The white walls. The bars. The fear. The emptiness. The loneliness. Her lost childhood.

She is sobbing because everything is starting to come back to her. Her marriage. Her children. Her friends. Her life. The Soiree. The shots…eight shots. Eight shots. Her dad. The man at the party. "My dad is dead. It is my fault. It is all my fault."

The nurse enters just as William pulls her off of him. He grabs both of her arms. Looks her in the eyes. "Karen, LOOK AT ME. It's not your fault. The person who killed your dad is at fault. You were a child." He lets go of Karen as the nurse grabs his arm signaling for him to let go of Karen. So he steps back and walks out of the room. Peaches follows behind him.

The nurse can be heard saying, "Okay, Mrs. Lime. The doctor wants you to take this medication to help with the anxiety. You're okay."

Peaches and William stand in the hall. Peaches is confused. "William, what is going on with her? I thought this was because of the murder at my party but this is some other shit."

Shaking his head, William replies, "Yes! Yes, it is. There is a lot. I have been dealing with Karen and her trauma for a while. Her dad was murdered in front of her when she was eight.

I think the shooting at your party triggered something in her."

Peaches gasps, "Oh my goodness. I had no idea. I feel so bad for her."

"Yea; I know. It's a lot to deal with. I am surprised that she never told you."

"Humph! I'm sure she blocked this out of her mind. Wouldn't you?" Peaches gives a slight laugh. "You need to go get the kids. I will stay with her. I will call you if the doctor needs you. Someone needs to make sure that she is getting what she needs. Let me see if they will get me a chair."

"Thank you Peaches." William gives her a hug. "You are a true friend and that is what she needs right now. Let me tell her that I am leaving. Please give me a call when the doctor comes to talk to her. We need to make sure everything is as normal as possible for the sake of the kids."

"Understood."

William goes back into the room and tells Karen that he is going to get the children. He reassures her that he will return soon or she will be home soon. Karen is satisfied with his answer so she lays back and lets the medicine kick in.

After William leaves, the nurse brings in a chair for Peaches to sit in. Karen wakes up and finds her friend

Peaches sitting beside her watching a movie on her phone.

"Hey Peaches! Has William been back yet?"

"No girl. Stop worrying about that man." Peaches laughs. "We are worried about you getting up out of here. He is with Willow and Will J."

"You're right. I'm sorry. I'm sorry about your party."

"You're sorry for what? There will be other parties. It is unfortunate that men have to be men and cannot solve their problems without their fists or guns."

"I know." Karen whispers, "Eight shots."

"What did you say?" Peaches asks concerned.

"I said it was eight shots." Karen puts her head down.

Peaches asks, "Eight shots? What does that mean?"

"He shot my dad eight times. The man at The Winston shot that man eight times." A tear falls down Karen's face.

"That is a coincidence. You never told me that your dad was murdered."

"Yes. My dad was murdered." Karen wipes the tear from her cheek. The pain turns to anger. "Because of my mother, Lordess. Lordess, the Queen of the Cubs."

"Oh my! Your mom killed your dad?" Peaches asks.

"Not directly." Karen adds. "She might as well have pulled the trigger."

"What do you mean?"

"Let me tell you all about what my mother did after my father was murdered." Karen starts to tell Peaches her story about Lordess, Queen of the Cubs.

***

After Kevin died, Lordess had no choice but to turn to Oscar. Lordess needs a man in her life because she never worked. Cubs don't work. She needs Oscar and Oscar knows this.

Oscar was "The Man" and was well known in the area. After all he was the local drug distro. Ever since word in the streets was that he had Kevin shot dead in broad daylight in front of a school, everybody was afraid of him. Only a crazy man would do something like that.

Oscar made life a living hell for both Lordess and Karen. When Oscar came home, he would always force Lordess to go into the bedroom with him. He would force her to either have sex with him or perform some sexual act with him.

He was verbally abusive to both Karen and Lordess. As for Karen, he was physically abusive towards her. It was almost like he hated her.

"O" would spank Karen just for side eyeing him. He always seemed to find a reason to put his hands on her.

122

Any hint of disrespect from Karen, was met with a blow to the side of her head or a belt to her backside. Horrified, Lordess would just sit there and wait for it all to end. Then she would comfort her daughter when it was over but she never stood up against Oscar. Lordess was all that Karen had. So she had no choice but to endure the abuse. She didn't want her mom to get into any trouble. She couldn't lose her mom either.

Oscar would call Lordess names to remind her of how stupid she is. Then tell her things about her appearance to make her feel unattractive. He would say, "Shut up stupid bitch! Where the f*** are you going to go? Look at you. You getting old. Don't nobody want your old ass but me."

One day Oscar came home drunk. That day he let it slip out. Oscar let it slip that he had murdered Kevin. He summoned Lordess to the bedroom. She went in and Karen sat at the kitchen table finishing up her homework.

When Lordess came out of the bedroom, she was crying.

"Mom?" Karen said in a manner of asking if she was okay."

Lordess understood and she smiled back without a word. She went to the stove and continued to stir the pot of pasta on the stove.

Then Oscar comes into the kitchen. Oscar is so drunk that he is staggering around. He walks up behind Lordess and starts kissing her neck. She tries to pull away because he is pressing her up against the hot stove. Patiently, she says, "Give me a minute O. I need to finish this pasta to get dinner on the table for Karen."

"Forget her." Stumbling he says as he looks at Karen. "What are you looking at brat?"

Karen puts her head down to look at her homework because she knows what could come next. She doesn't say a word.

Oscar stumbles over to her. He puts both hands on the table, which makes Karen lookup. He says, "Unbreakable, huh?" He burst out laughing. "Unbreakable!" He pulls out an imaginary gun and starts shooting. "Pow! Pow! Pow! Pow! Pow! Pow! Pow!" Oscar cocks back an imaginary gun, "POOOOWWWWW!"

Karen stares at him trembling in horror, hitting her left fist to her left thigh.

Oscar bursts out laughing again. "Eight shots for you baby girl. Eight shots all for you." He stands there in the middle of the kitchen posed like he was that day, smiling. Smiling at Lordess and smiling at Karen.

Karen was horrified, "YOU KILLED MY DAD!"

Lordess drops the pasta spoon that she was holding. She cannot believe what she has just heard. Of course she heard what the streets had to say but Oscar reassured her, "It's just the streets talkin'." She could not believe what he confessed. *How could he do that to me? I made a mess of everything. My life. My daughter's life all because I wanted to live a certain lifestyle and I couldn't forgive my husband for being a man when he cheated on me. Lord, please forgive me.* "Oscar, did you really?"

Oscar swaying back and forth, "Yes I killed that nigga. He was in the way. When something gets in my way, I eliminate it. I gave you a choice that morning. I told you to leave him and you said you couldn't so I made the choice for you."

Lordess just shakes her head, disappointed.

"Now that you know the truth, let's get some things straight. I know a lot of people and if I go to jail, neither of you will ever be safe. Do you understand me?" Oscar asks.

Lordess looks at Karen and then at Oscar. They both shake their heads yes.

"Good. Good. That's my good girls." Oscar is pleased.

Karen never testifies against Oscar. Then apparently no one else at the school would testify to seeing anything. So Kevin's murder was left unsolved.

Karen did not want her mother to be upset and lonely. Karen knew that her mother needed a companion so she was obedient and did not cause problems for Oscar and Lordess. Plus, she was also afraid of what Oscar would do to her and her mother.

Karen watched her mom go through trauma and not get the

help she needed. Karen watched her mother suffer in silence and isolate herself from family and friends.

Lordess was slowly letting her guilt consume her. Oscar had imprisoned her. Oscar did not want her or Karen to talk to anyone because he was afraid they would tell someone what he did. He had people watching Lordess' every move. His paranoia got worse and he started accusing Lordess of cheating on him. So much so that he started physically abusing her.

Over the years, Lordess had been teaching Karen how to be a Cub. Because she got thrown off her game, she vowed to teach Karen how to play the game better than her. Over the years, she would tell Karen, "When you are with a man or when a man likes you, don't you ever take out your wallet. Don't ever offer to pay for anything. Men don't care nothin' about how smart you are. They only care about how submissive you can be and how good you look on their arm."

When Lordess was convinced that Karen knew the game and that Karen could take care of herself in this cruel world. That is when she decided to put her plan into action.

She knows that Oscar's men are watching her every move. Every week she makes plans for some of her friends to meet her in various places such as the grocery store, a restaurant, the post office, a utility company, a convenience store, and Karen's school. Lordess would bring things that belong to Karen and pass it on to the friend that is meeting

126

her. Slowly Lordess moved Karen out of the house.

Finally, the day comes. Lordess goes up to the school to pick up Karen and her school records. One of Lordess' friends, Sierra, from D.C., meets her at the school. Lordess tells Oscar that she has a meeting with one of Karen's teachers.

At the school, she explains to the principal and her teacher that Karen must leave the state and no one must know that she withdrew. The principal doesn't ask any questions. It is like he already knows. He tells the guidance counselor to release Karen's records.

The secretary calls Karen down to the office. When Karen arrives in the front office, she is so happy to see her mother there waiting for her. Karen begins to run to her mother but stops to look around to see who is watching. The last time she ran to a parent changed her entire life.

Lordess notes her daughter's hesitation, "It is okay Sweetheart. He won't hurt you anymore."

Karen embraces her mom with one of the tightest hugs she has ever given.

For Lordess, it felt as if her daughter knew something was about to happen. "Hey Honey! This is my friend Sierra. Do you remember her?"

Karen shakes her head yes. *Why does mom want me to meet this lady?*

"Karen, I love you very much but I am afraid for your life. I have to get you away from Oscar before he kills me or you or both of us. I cannot leave right now but Sierra is prepared to take you now. I will join you later."

"No Mommy! I don't want to go without you. I'm scared."

"What? My brave little Cub is scared? Nooooo! Sierra has come to take you to D.C. You are going to have so much fun. Just think of all of the places that you can visit."

Karen is getting angry and frustrated. She starts hitting her left hand to left thigh. She pushes Lordess back. She starts yelling, "ALL of this is your fault. If you hadn't decided to cheat, NONE of this would have happened. You are selfish, manipulative conniving and I HATE you. YOU are the reason my dad is dead. You are DEAD to me, Lordess."

Everyone is shocked. They cannot believe the words that are coming from quiet Karen's mouth.

Softly, Lordess says, "I am sorry that you feel that way. Hopefully one day you will change your mind. But for now you must go with Sierra. I will join you in D.C. as soon as I can." Lordess walks away with tears in her eyes. She turns back around to Karen. "I love you, my little cub. Don't forget that and always remember everything that I taught you. "*No regales la leche por gratis*", Spanish translation of "don't give away the milk for free." Lordess blows a kiss at Karen and leaves.

As Sierra and Karen walk slowly to the car, Sierra says,

"We have a long drive ahead of us. But that is okay. That will give us a chance to really get to know each other." Sierra opens the door to the backseat.

Karen stops in awe.

In the backseat of the car, are all of Karen's most prized possessions. The framed picture of her and her dad. A picture of Karen and Lordess. The green elephant that her dad gave her when she was three. Her favorite blanket and pillow. A basket full of her favorite foods and drinks. And laying on top of the pillow is the ballerina mirror. The mirror that her dad had for her in that pink bag that sat in his blood on that dreadful day. Karen loved that mirror. That was the last thing her dad ever gave her.

"Surprise!" Sierra screams, "Your mom did this for you. Your mom has been working on getting you out of here for a while. She loves you Karen. We all do. A lot of people have been trying to make this happen for you. We will come back for your mom. Don't worry."

Karen felt bad for all of the terrible things that she had said to her mom. She wishes she could take them back…Well some of them. But nine-year-old Karen knew the difference between right and wrong. She vowed that if she ever got married, she would never cheat on her husband. She would always keep her family together *by any means necessary.*

Later on that night when Oscar got home, he found police cars lined up in front of his house and a distraught Lordess crying hysterically. He started to get angry because he thought that Lordess or Karen had called the police and snitched about his secret.

Lordess ran up to him sobbing, "Karen ran away." She grabs hold of him and cries in his shirt.

Oscar tries to console her as he tries to hide his contentment. *Now I can have the family that I wanted. Karen is gone. And Lordess is pregnant with my baby. Everything's coming together.*

***

Peaches is stunned. She sits there quietly waiting for Karen to finish her story.

"Sierra and I drove the twenty-two-hour drive from Houston to D.C. We talked, laughed and cried. We stopped in different places. Ate at famous restaurants. It was the best trip I have ever had." Karen paused, "Sierra made me feel love like I hadn't felt in a long time."

"You needed that trip Karen after all that you had been through." Peaches wiped some of the tears from her eyes. "How could your mom look at Oscar knowing that he killed your father?"

"I think deep inside she knew. She just didn't want to admit it to herself."

"Well I am sure things got better when she finally got away from him and moved up here with you. Right?"

130

Karen laughs, "She never moved up here. She gave me to Sierra. Sierra raised me."

"What? After her elaborate plan to get you out of Houston, you mean to tell me that she never moved up here? Please explain."

"It's simple. She got pregnant. In fact, she was pregnant when she sent me away and she never mentioned it." Karen laughs. "Not one word."

"Did you ever see her again?"

"Yes, I have seen her a few times. She has come up here a few times over the years but once I found out that she had a baby with Oscar, I didn't want anything to do with her. She is really dead to me."

"WOW!!! The nerve." Peaches is astonished.

"She said it was all to protect me. She even brought Sergio with her."

"Who is Sergio?" Asks Peaches.

"He is my little brother that she had with Oscar. You know if I didn't want to see her. I dang sure didn't want to meet him especially since she couldn't tell him who I was. Lordess couldn't tell Oscar that she knew where I was or that she was in contact with me."

Peaches now understands Karen a bit more. Karen has experienced some major trauma. That is why she acted the way she did at the party. "Karen, I feel so bad for you. You have been through some real shit girl."

"Not to mention the fact that I have an older brother that Lordess would not let me meet. My dad wasn't even allowed to talk about him. His name is KJ. But we could never talk about him."

The doctor comes in and interrupts the conversation. "How are you today Mrs. Lime?'

"I am feeling fine, doctor. I am just ready to go home." Karen says, perking up.

"Good! I spoke to your regular doctor. It seems that he has been treating you for mild anxiety and situational depression."

"Yes doctor. I have been experiencing anxiety and depression since I was in middle school."

"Well after speaking to your regular physician, we have decided to slightly increase the dosage of your medication. We would also like for you to see a psychiatrist and continue with your regular therapy appointments. Are you taking your medication regularly?"

"Yes! Everyday." Karen states proudly.

In reality, Karen is delusional. Like many people she never went to the doctor to be accurately diagnosed. Due to her childhood traumas she has a habit of detaching herself from her emotions and other times she felt numb to her emotions because she knew that she wanted to keep her family together. There were times when she could not remember where she had been or who she had been with. Sometimes it was like she was watching a movie of her life.

"Okay Karen! I will have the nurse process your discharge papers. Go ahead and get dressed. Is your pretty little friend here going to take you home?"

Peaches blushes at the handsome doctor.

Karen ignoring the flirting interactions, "Yes, she is going to take me home."

"Great! If you have any questions or concerns, please feel free to call me." The doctor passes his business card to Peaches.

"We sure will." Peaches says smiling, as she retrieves the card from the doctor's hand.

"Talk to you soon ladies."

Karen jumps out of the bed and runs around looking for her clothes.

"Whoa! Slow down Karen. I have your clothes. William brought you some clothes. I have them right here." She passes Karen her clothes.

Karen quickly puts her clothes on and takes a seat on the edge of the bed ready to go. "I just know my hair is a mess. I need to call Lou."

"Well William has your phone so you can't call anyone right now."

The nurse comes in with the discharge papers and a wheelchair. Karen plops down in the wheelchair, excited to go home to her family.

I know William and the kids are home anxiously waiting for me. We can watch a movie together like a family. Unbreakable...nothing is going to come between me and my family.

"The funny thing about the heart is a soft heart is a strong heart, and a hard heart is a weak heart."— Criss Jami, Healology

Chapter VIII: The Illegitimate Response

Unwanted Input

Peaches pulls up in front of Karen's house.

Karen is so excited when she sees that William's truck is there. "Look Peaches. He is here. My hubby is here waiting for me."

Karen leaps out of the car leaving Peaches to grab her things from the car.

Karen walks into the house and shouts, "I'M HOME!"

There is silence. No one comes running. No one is stirring until Peaches comes in the door. "Where is everybody?" Peaches asks.

Karen is puzzled. "Hello? Mommy is home." She stops to look in the mirror to adjust her hair. "Where is my family?"

"We are here. We are all here in the kitchen. William says."

Karen and Peaches walk into the kitchen. The Lime family is sitting at the table eating pizza. No one looks up.

Will J looks up from his game, "Hey Mom!" Then he looks back down.

Willow and William never look up. "Hey!" They say monotone and in unison.

"Hello my beautiful family. Did you miss mommy while she was at the spa?" Karen asks.

Everyone looks at Karen like she is crazy thinking…*What spa?* However, only one person is bold enough to say it.

"The spa?" Willow says, looking at her mother as if she has two heads. "I thought you were in the looney bin."

William nudges Willow.

Willow turns her nose up at him and mouths, "What?"

Peaches turns away pretending to look at a picture on the wall.

Will J continues to eat his pizza and play his game.

Karen bursts out laughing. "Willow, you are so funny. Why no dear. I was at the spa. I got a full body massage. Then I got the 10 Karat gold facial. Look at my skin." Karen puts her face down close to Willow's. She uses the back of her right hand and glides it over her right cheek. "See how smooth my face is?"

"Mom, we are not stupid. Daddy already told us what happened. Stop lying. Just tell the truth. Dang." Willow is

136

frustrated.

"On that note," Peaches interrupts. "I am leaving. Karen, I will call you before I come by."

Karen reaches out for a hug. "Thank you so much Peaches. You are such a great friend. I will see you tomorrow."

"William, kids, if you need anything, you know how to reach me." Peaches heads towards the door.

William yells after Peaches, "Thank you! See you later."

The children yell, "Bye Auntie Peaches."

"I guess I better be leaving to Karen." William stands up and throws away his plate.

Karen was disappointed, "But William, I thought you were staying the night."

"No Karen. I have a home. I thought that you and the kids could spend time together. You know, get back to your usual routine."

"But…"

William can see that Karen is getting upset. He walks over to her and looks her in the eyes, "Listen Karen, I will be here in the morning to pick the kids up for school. Then I will take them for the weekend so that you can get some rest. When you are ready, we will have a talk about the future of our family. Is that fair?"

"That is fair William." Karen smiles.

William kisses her gently on the cheek. "I will see you in the morning. Willow, Will J. I will see you in the morning. Make sure you have your clothes packed in your weekend bags. I love you guys."

William leaves and there is an awkward silence among Karen and her two children.

Karen looks over at her children. *Oh my goodness! I love these two so much. I would never let anyone harm them physically, mentally or emotionally. Have I done that to them? Have I abused my children like Lordess did to me or the way she let "O" abuse me?*

At that moment, she had a revelation. She did not want her kids to experience the traumas she had as a child. Lordess never sought help for her and Karen never sought help for her traumas.

Karen realized that her traumas put a toll on her marriage. She tried to keep it together by denying that there was a problem. She did not want to talk to anyone because she knew she was fine. She believed nothing was wrong with her or her family. But now after this latest incident she knew that she was not fine.

She decides that she needs to let her children know about her traumas. *They need to know why I am the way that I am. It is time for a heart to heart talk with Willow and William J. I am going to tell them what I went through as a*

138

child. She never told them.

She felt like they didn't like her as a mother. I don't think they really know me as a mother.

"Hey kids! Can we go into the living room? I need to talk to you all about some things."

"Now?" Willow asks with an attitude.

"Yes now. I think it is time that we talk. I have some things that I need to explain to you all."

"Okay!" Will J. says, happily and heads to the living room.

Karen follows along behind him and looks back at Willow.

Willow sucks her teeth and follows behind Karen into the living room and flops down on the sofa. "Go ahead mom."

Karen takes a deep breath and starts telling her story. "I want to start my story by telling you that I love you two very much. Everything that I have done is because I have tried to protect you from experiencing some of the terrible things that I experienced as a child."

Willow interrupts, "Is that why you are always talking to yourself? You are trying to protect us?"

Karen laughs, "No Sweetheart. What are you talking about? I don't talk to myself. You must be mistaken. I must be on the phone."

139

"Yes you do Mom." Willow changes to a calm tone. "Will J. sees it too. You start laughing and talking to yourself. It scares us. You need to get some help Mom. I hope that the new meds that the doctor gave you will help but we are really worried."

"Let me tell my story first, Willow. Then maybe we can talk about that." Karen ignores what her daughter has to say. *I don't talk to myself.*

Karen starts her story. The story of her life from her perspective; her rose colored glasses.

***

I have two brothers. Kevin Jr. or KJ. That is what my dad used to call him, my father's son. Then there is Sergio, my younger brother from my mother. Since she sent me away, I never got a chance to meet him.

All this time, Willow thought Karen was an only child. "Why haven't we met our uncles or anyone else on your side of the family?"

"I have never met either one of them." Karen says. "And I do not talk to my mother. She had my father killed."

"WHAT?" Will J. says. "Grandma doesn't seem like a nice person."

"She was a tyrant." Tears start to well up in Karen's eyes and her voice starts to tremble. "I never felt loved by her. She always made me feel like I was a burden to her."

Karen's story:

My dad's name was Kevin. He wanted to name me Kevina but my mother said it was too ethnic so they named me Karen. Lordess said Karen is a neutral name so when people saw my name they didn't immediately label me as black, white or Hispanic.

My dad and Lordess met in high school. They fell in love. Then they got married. But before they started dating, my dad had a girlfriend named Sophia. She tried to trap my dad because he was about to get drafted into the NBA. She got pregnant but my dad didn't want to marry her. Sophia kept trying to get my dad to see this baby but my dad refused to see the child because he didn't think that it was his baby. Plus, he had me so he didn't need another child.

Then one day Sophia got my dad to come over to her house. She drugged him and made him cheat on my mom. My dad was so ashamed. He begged my mother to forgive him but she wouldn't. She felt betrayed so then she went off and got a boyfriend named Oscar, but I called him "O". He was a horrible man.

"O" had this hold over my mother. She just could not escape him. He was too powerful. Then one day he demanded that my mother leave my dad. She told him that she could not do that. She had made vows to my dad. "Till death do us part?" Oscar told her, "Then he must die. You have to kill him."

So Oscar and Lordess came up with this elaborate scheme to kill my dad. First, Lordess got my dad to pick me up from school and take me to the circus. She convinced my dad that it would be a great daddy/daughter day trip. My dad agreed and went to pick me up at school. Little did my dad know but Lordess and Oscar were already there…waiting.

Lordess sat in the car while my dad waited for me in front of the school. Oscar was standing there beside him. I had known Oscar as one of my mom's friends but at the time I did not know that he was her boyfriend.

When I saw my dad, I got so excited because I loved my dad so much. He treated me like I was a princess. He always made me feel loved and valued. I took off running towards him. Then all of a sudden Oscar pushed him down and shot him like 20 times. He was screaming, "This is for Lordess." Then he took off running to a car that had pulled up. When I looked inside the car, I saw my mom, laughing. She was driving the getaway car. She just left me standing there.

I ended up in the hospital for a few days. I actually stayed there until the funeral. Lordess came to see me in the hospital. She acted so distraught and sad. Then at the funeral, she was falling out crying. Everybody was coming up to us both, hugging us and consoling us. I was numb. I couldn't tell anyone what happened.

Sophia tried to bring KJ to the funeral but Lordess refused

to allow them to attend. Again, she kept me from meeting my big brother. I didn't want to meet him anyway. It was his fault and Sophia's fault that my dad was dead. If Sophia hadn't drugged my dad, Lordess never would have got with that man Oscar.

Then that next week we moved into Oscar's house. My life was horrible. Oscar hated me and he beat me every day just for being me. Lordess didn't do a thing to help me. She just watched. Then one day I just ran away. I knew they were tired of me. Lordess didn't want me anymore. Next thing I know she was having Oscar's baby. She had replaced me.

When I got here to DC, I reached out to Lordess. Lordess tried to get me to meet Sergio but I refused to meet him. She had told Oscar that I was dead so she couldn't introduce me to Sergio as his big sister. Sergio would just know me as some random little girl that he met in DC.

"So now you have it…my story. If it hadn't been for Miss Sierra, I never would have had the opportunities that I have been given by God. To feel loved, to be a mother. I never experienced that with my mother." Karen looks at her children. "I hope this helps you two understand a little more about me and why I do some of the things that I do. I have been a victim most of my life. I cannot control some of my actions but I am working on myself. If you talk to your dad, let him know that I am changing for us. Our family."

Karen puts her face in her hands and starts bawling her

eyes out. Will J gives his mom a hug and rubs her back. On the other hand, there is Willow…

***

Willow sat in silence and listened to her mother's story and watched her mom's crocodile tears streaming from face. Part of her wants to believe that her mother endured all of this abuse but the other part of her realizes that her mother's point of view is not always logical nor is it realistic. *Why can't we meet our grandmother? Where does she live? I need to get to the bottom of this.*

Karen sits with her face in her hands but at the same time she is watching Willow through her fingers. She can see Willow. She can sense that Willow has more questions. She can see the wheels turning in Willows head. Willow is not going to tell William anything. *Willow is my problem. Willow keeps saying that Will J. is not Williams. How can she say that?*

"Synchronicity occurs at the intersection of your awareness, response, perspective, and action." — *Andrea Goeglein*

Chapter IX: *The Gatekeeper*

Control Access

Willow snatches open the door to her dad's Jeep and flops down into the seat, exhausted.

Looking at her awkwardly, William asks, "Good Morning! What is wrong with you? Was it a long night with your mother?"

Rolling her eyes, Willow huffs, "Ugghhhh! Was it ever? Daddy I just don't know what to think. Mom is all over the place. She told us this long as–" She stops herself in mid-sentence because she almost forgot that she was talking to her dad and not her friends. "Sorry Dad. She told us this long story about her childhood and her brothers. Did she really see her dad murdered by her mom?"

William thinks a minute before he answers his daughter. William loves Karen but he can no longer deal with her behavior. Ever since he has known her he has provided for her and made sure that she had everything that they needed. He dealt with her mental and emotional issues. Her traumas. He supported her in everything. He ignored her erratic actions. He was tired. *Now how do I answer my daughter's questions?*

"Well I believe it was something like that. I am not sure if her mother was actually there. I just think your mother feels that her mother is responsible for her father's death. Yes, she does have two brothers, but she doesn't have a relationship with them. No matter what your mom tells you long story short…your mom had a traumatic childhood and as a result it sometimes affects her adult life."

"Is that why she talks to herself?" Willow asks. "Is that why you left us? Is Miss Charlice your new girlfriend? Is that why Will J. doesn't look like any of us?" Willow looks straight at her dad to see his reaction to her last question.

William locks eyes with his daughter. At that moment, Will J. gets into the Jeep. Willow and William's eyes unlock. "Hey buddy!" William turns to the back to look at his son. Then turns back to Willow who is still looking at him waiting for an answer. "Look Willow we can talk about this later but I will say I love BOTH of MY children. I have been there with you from day one and I always will be. Do you understand?"

Willow shrugs her shoulders like whatever. Rolls her eyes, puts on her headphones and turns the music up on her phone. *I am over this conversation.* Willow wanted answers but Will J had interrupted. She has always felt that her dad favored Will J over her. *Is it because he is a boy or is it because he is light skinned? Or is it because Will J's real dad is dead like mom's dad? Maybe mom killed Will J's dad.* Willow laughs at that idea. *Some of my mom has rubbed off on me.*

William drops his children off in front of their school. "Have a nice day! I will be here to pick you up at dismissal. You will be spending the weekend with me. Love you!"

Willow hops out the Jeep without saying a word and slams the door. She never looks back. She just walks straight towards the school. Some of her friends are calling her name but she just keeps walking ahead.

On the other hand, Will J reaches in the front seat, gives his dad a huge hug and says, "I love you too Daddy. See you after school." He then hops out, closes the door and runs down the sidewalk to catch up with Willow.

William just sits in his Jeep watching his children until they disappear into the school. What is he going to do with thirteen-year-old Willow? She is growing up so fast. She is intelligent and she has questions that he's not even sure that he can answer.

Just then, William's phone rings. It is Charlice. "Hey Babe!" He answers.

"Hey handsome! Did you get the kids to school this morning? Did you let them know that I would be around this weekend?" Charlice asks.

"We never made it that far in the conversation. That Willow kept asking me questions. I was not prepared to answer her. Now is not the time."

"What do you mean William? Now is not the time. What did she want to know?"

"Of course, she asked about my relationship with you. Then she asked why I left the family. Then she wanted to know about Will J."

Charlice anxiously asks, "Well what did you tell her about us? Did you tell her that you left because you don't want to be with her mother? What did you say, William?"

"I didn't say anything Charlice. Will J got in the truck? I couldn't answer questions about him, especially since I couldn't answer them."

"Why couldn't you answer questions about Will J? He's your son right?"

William takes a deep breath.

"Hello William? Are you there?" Charlice pauses. "Did you hear me?"

"For ten years, I have had my doubts about Will J being my son. First of all, look at him. He is damn near white with thick curly hair. He actually resembles her ex-boyfriend from high school. A few times in our marriage Karen has had these episodes where she goes off. She just disappears. She hasn't done it that much since the children have gotten older but she used to do it pretty often. She says she cannot remember where she was or what she did. I don't know

148

what to believe. I was so happy when we found out that she was pregnant with our son. But when he came out, we were so confused. Karen and I are both dark skinned and here comes our high yellow baby. She told me that he would get darker as he got older." William laughs. "But I am still waiting for his skin to darken up ten years later."

Charlice laughs too, "Well you know we come in all shades of black. Color is not hereditary."

"I know but like I said, he looks like her ex-boyfriend. She was probably with him during one of her black out episodes. I love my son though. I have always wanted a son. I wouldn't trade him for anything. They are the reason I stay in Karen's life."

The children are actively involved in extracurricular activities. This is what held the Lime family together. Obligation. This was the baggage William held on to. He really wanted to wait until the kids were grown before leaving but his whole life would be gone. That is why he decided that he had to leave.

"Okay!" Charlice says, "Since you have your doubts, go buy a DNA test at the drug store."

William hesitates, "I don't know Charlice. This could change a lot of things. What if he is not mine?"

"William, you need to be 100 percent sure. This isn't just for you. It is for Will J as well. He needs to know." Charlice urges William.

"Hold on Charlice. Will J. is calling my phone." William clicks the phone over. "Hello Will J?"

Will J can be heard crying on the other end of the phone. "Daddy?"

"Yes Will J. What is wrong Buddy? Talk to Daddy."

"Daddy, Willow has been mean to me all day. Willow says that you are not my dad. Why would she say that Dad?" Will J pauses to sob into the phone. He is so upset. "She says I don't look anything like you or her or mom. Daddy, is it true? Are you my dad?"

"Of course, I am your dad Will J. Don't be silly. Stop crying. I will see you after school. You, Willow and I will have a nice deep conversation. Love you."

"Okay Daddy." Will J is relieved. "I will see you after school. Love you, Dad. Best Daddy in the world."

William clicks back over to Charlice, "Okay! What do I need to do to take this test?"

"You buy the kit. You swab the inside of your mouth. Then you swab Will J's mouth. Then you put the used swabs in containers and you send it off to the lab. The results should be back in about 30 days. Voila! You will have your answer in 30 days from the date you mail the swabs."

"I will do it. I will do the test while Karen is on her vacation cruise. That is the perfect time to do it. Let me give you a call later. I am going to the drugstore now."

William has made up his mind.

William reflects. *Will J looks nothing like me. I know this.* William has been hoping and praying that William Jr. is his but it's too far-fetched. William is drained just thinking that William Jr. may not be his son. William knows that now is the time to talk to his children about everything they are feeling but he doesn't know how. *I have to have these results first. Once I have these results, I will have an open and honest conversation with my children.*

William thought many times of how he could protect his children. Every decision that he had made was to protect his children from experiencing pain like both him and Karen had experienced as children. Now he felt guilty. He felt like he had abandoned them. He had left them with their mother who was not well mentally. *I have to convince Karen to get some help for the sake of the children. They don't deserve to live like this. I have to make this right.*

"Now how the hell do I convince Karen to get help?" William shakes his head and proceeds to drive to the drug store.

On the way to the drugstore, he calls Karen. "Hey Karen! How are you feeling today?"

"Good Morning Dear! I feel WONDERFUL! I called Lou to let her know that I am coming in today. My hair looks a mess. Going to the spa really messed up my hair." Karen sounds so chipper and relaxed.

"Um Karen…" William starts carefully choosing his words. "You were not at a spa. You were at the hospital. You were in the psychiatric ward at Howard University Hospital. Do you remember what happened at the Gala?"

Karen is silent for a minute. She laughs. "Yes Dear! My Dad got shot. I mean that man got shot in front of the hotel. I remember. Then I fainted and went to the spa to clear my mind. I remember everything."

"Karen, you did NOT go to the spa. You went to the hospital. You were found screaming in a corner outside of the hotel. They called an ambulance to come get you and you were placed in the psychiatric ward. Do you remember now?" William is getting a little irritated with Karen's denial.

Karen burst into a hysterical laughter. "I know dear but I cannot tell people that. I was at the spa. That is my story."

William does not find Karen's story amusing. "Karen, despite your version of the story, you need to go to therapy. I know you may disagree but just a few nights in the psych ward are not enough. You need to deal with these traumatic events from your past."

"Will, I don't understand why you are so worried. I saw a man get shot. Who else wouldn't duck down and scream?" Karen brushes off his concerns.

"Yes, Karen," frustrated William takes a breath, "people do duck down when they hear shots." He takes another deep breath, "However, mentally stable people do not ball up in the corner screaming daddy, daddy, daddy. You did that Karen. YOU did that. No one else went to the psych ward. Only you did, Karen."

Karen thinks for a moment. Then she goes off. "Are you accusing me of being mentally unstable? How can you say that to me?" She starts to sob. "Are you sure no one else went to the hospital? Are you REALLY sure?"

William has to back track. "I am sorry Karen. I apologize. I didn't mean to upset you. It's just that I am concerned about you. I am concerned about the kids and about our family." He knows exactly what to say to calm her down. *Just mention the family and us working things out.* "I want what is best for us. You need to attend counseling. You need to talk to someone. Will you try counseling?"

Karen thinks for a moment. She is unsure of what she should do. She wants to talk it over with someone. *Ahh Peaches! I will call Peaches.* "Dear, I will think about it and get back to you. Enjoy your weekend with the kids. Bye!" She hangs up the phone. She is tired of going back and forth with him.

Karen wanted to talk it over with Peaches. Because Peaches showed up at the hospital, she felt like she could trust Peaches…just a little. *What kind of help do I possibly need? Help? Humph! What kind of help does William want me to get? I know we need help with our marriage and maybe I need help building a better relationship with*

Willow and William Jr. "I don't know what he wants from me."

Karen thought. *If I build a better relationship with Willow and William Jr, then my relationship with William will improve.* "We can be a family again. Peaches will know what to do. Let me call her." She calls Peaches.

"Hey girl! How are you doing today?" Peaches was glad to hear from Karen. She had forgotten to call her to check on her. She was having a busy day.

She was a little busy trying to get all the necessary paperwork together for the girls' getaway cruise. Fourteen days is a long time to be away from the city and work. There were so many minor details that had to be taken care of before she left. She has to put people in place before she leaves. She does not want to be disturbed on this vacay. She needed everything to go extremely well especially after the unfortunate incident at the All White Gala. Peaches cringed just thinking about the whole night.

One thing she had to make sure of was that her cruise goers were capable of handling this excursion. Peaches has to ensure that Karen is good physically and mentally.

"Hey Peaches! I am well. In fact, I am about to get dressed and go to see Lou. My hair is just horrid from being at the spa."

Peaches is confused. She looks at her phone. "The spa? When did you have time to go to the spa? You just came

154

home from the hospital yesterday. I drove you remember? Did you go to the spa this morning?"

Karen laughs, "Yes, I was able to squeeze in some time at the spa. I just had to get my mind right."

"Oh good! I am so glad that you were able to fit some "Me Time" into your schedule. So with that being said, do you think you are up to going on the cruise? Especially because of all you have been through over the last week."

"Yes! Oh yes! I would not miss the cruise for the world. William needs some time to miss me and to contemplate our next move. Speaking of William, he just asked me if I would go get some help. Isn't that silly? What do I need help for? There is nothing wrong with me." Karen waits for her good friend's response.

Peaches chooses her words carefully. She knows Karen and right now Karen is emotionally sensitive. After her talk with William, she understands Karen a little bit better. "Karen, everyone should go to therapy. Hell, I've gone to therapy. The beautiful thing about therapy is that you get to talk to someone who doesn't know you or your family. They are neutral and can help you look at situations from a different perspective. It can't hurt can it?"

"No you are right. I'm just not sure why he wants to go?" Karen needs more convincing.

"Perhaps he wants marriage counseling. Do you think he wants to work on your marriage? It's about time. Geesh!"

155

"I never thought about that. I had asked before and he was against it. Maybe after the incident, he realized how important I am to him." Karen gets excited.

Trying not to get her hopes up too high Peaches offers another suggestion. "Maybe he wants to do family counseling to work on your family. Or maybe he just wants you all to do individual counseling just to see if you all can each work on yourselves. I have just the person for you to get in touch with. Her name is Dr. Wells. She is a family counselor. There I just text you her contact information. She is wonderful."

"I will give her a call now. Thank you Peaches. I appreciate your help. You always come through for me." Karen is so glad that she talked to Peaches.

"Anytime girl. That's what friends are for. Okay! I gotta run. I'm still putting out these fires from the Gala. We will talk later. Love you! MWAH!" Peaches ends the call.

***

Karen wastes no time and calls Dr. Well's office. She reaches Dr. Wells' answering service. "Hi Dr. Wells. My name is Karen Lime. I am a friend of Peaches. She suggested that I give you a call to set up an appointment for family counseling. Please give me a call at your earliest convenience. My number is 301-555-8687. I look forward to hearing from you. Bye!"

Karen walks up and down her bedroom floor. "We don't

need family counseling. William and I need marriage counseling. Dr. Wells is a family counselor. If she returns my call, I will just let her know that we do not require her services. I will let her know that all I need is a good marriage counselor to help convince William to come back home and stop this foolishness."

In the meantime, Dr. Wells receives Karen's message and decides that she needs to call Karen. Dr. Wells normally handles high end clients but she decided to take on Karen and her family as a favor to Peaches. Dr. Wells knows that Peaches is well connected and she does not want to rock the boat with Peaches.

"Hello Mrs. Lime. This Dr. Wells returning your call. It seems that you are in need of family counseling. Can you tell me a little bit about yourself and your family so I can have a little background?"

"Hello, Dr. Wells. Thank you so much for returning my call. Actually I do not think that my family needs counseling. Actually my husband and I need marriage counseling. I thank Peaches for referring me to you but I do not think that we require your services."

"Well Mrs. Lime, family counseling includes marriage counseling. Not only do I provide therapy for the marriage couple, I provide counseling for the entire family when children are involved. Sometimes marriage counseling turns into family counseling AND individual counseling. Once we dive in, we often discover other issues and situations. Does that make sense?"

"Yes it does Dr. Wells." Karen.

"So give me a little background so we can determine how we need to start."

"Okay! So my husband, William and I have been together for almost 15 years. We have a 13-year-old daughter named Willow. Willow is a true teenager with all of the teenage girl emotions. William Jr. or Will J. is our 10-year-old son. He is just a little boy who loves his parents. Our children attend Sidwell Friends. I am a stay at home mom. I am a local socialite. I attend and help to organize all of the local events of the Who's Who in D.C."

Dr. Wells just listens to Karen. She is getting a sense of who this woman is. She is picking up on some of the narcissistic ideology of Karen. "Okay! And your husband? What about him?"

"My wonderful husband is a successful businessman who takes care of me. But for some reason he left us a few months ago. It has been almost a year. He tells me that he loves me. He does things with us as a family but he does not live with us. He moved in with a friend of his. A gay friend. I mean I don't think my Will is gay but he moved out. And I have no clue why he left us."

Dr. Wells asks, "If you don't mind me asking, when was the last time you and he were intimate?"

Karen is thrown off by the question. She hadn't thought about that. "Last week she answered. Yes. We have been intimate a few times since he moved out and the sex has been great. I don't mind sharing that. I'm just baffled as to why he doesn't want to live in our home."

Karen stops talking as she can hear Dr. Wells typing notes. "Okay Mrs. Lime, we need to set up two appointments. One for the entire family and one for you and William. When would you like to come in? I have some available appointments later next week in the evening so that it won't interfere with the children's school."

Karen has not confirmed with William. "Dr. Wells, can I get back with her after I speak with my husband? I need to confer with him to review his schedule."

"That is fine. Give my office a call and let my receptionist know what works best for you and I will see you and your family then."

"I will do that Dr. Wells. I look forward to meeting you. Goodbye! Thank you again." Karen is elated. She is not about to have someone on her side to help her convince William to come back home. "FINALLY!!" She screams and throws her arms up in the air like she just won a marathon.

Later on that evening William drops Willow off back and home. Willow walks in the door, side eyes her mom. "I forgot something." Then she runs upstairs to her room.

Karen walks out to William's Jeep. "Hey Will J. Are you guys coming in?"

"Hey Mom!" Will J. responds.

William looks over at Karen. "No, we have plans this evening. Willow forgot something. We will be gone in a flash."

"Well I wanted you to know that I found a counselor." Karen whispers.

"Oh great! When do you start?" William is excited. *She took the first step.*

"Well, that depends on you. I signed us up for marriage and family counseling." Karen smiles.

William looks at her like she has two heads. "Marriage counseling? Family counseling? That's not what we discussed. We discussed YOU needing counseling. Not us. Not our children."

"I hear what you are saying Dear. However, the therapist, Dr. Wells felt that in order for me to heal, the entire family needs to support me. She thought that perhaps the entire family could use some counseling due to my needs."

Just then Willow pushes past her mother and hops in the front seat of the Jeep. "I am ready Dad."

"Okay Karen! Let me think about it. Can you give me a few days to think about it?" William asks.

Karen is content. "Okay Dear! Just let me know. She is a well renowned therapist who has set aside time in her schedule to see us next Thursday or Friday so please let me know by Monday. Thanks! Love you guys! MWAH!" Karen walks away and does a happy dance up the driveway.

Willow and William turn to look at each other and shake their heads; bust out laughing. Then they drive off.

Later on that night Charlice comes to the house. Even though she technically lives with William, she stays in a hotel when the children are over. William feels that now is not the right time to introduce her to the children as his girlfriend. And it definitely isn't the appropriate time to let them know that she is living there.

William and Charlice are sitting in the living room enjoying each other's' company over a glass of wine. William and Charlice readdress the conversation he had with Willow. Charlice begins, "So have you and Willow talked again since this morning? Did you two finish your conversation?"

"No, we didn't get a chance. We were running around all evening. Willow had her dance class. She forgot something at the house so we had to run by there really quick. Then Karen started her antics again." William pronounce feeling sick to his stomach.

Charlice takes a sip of her wine. "What did she do now?" She asks.

"Well she has decided that she would like to get counseling for the children because they have been through so much with her behavior and with the break up." William looks over at Charlice to see her reaction. He only shares counseling for the children. He decided to leave out marriage counseling for now because he has already made up his mind that he and Karen are not getting back together so he didn't feel the need to include that part when he told Charlice.

Charlice, trying not to be selfish, tells William, "Do what's best for you and your family." Inside she is feeling a little uneasy. How long is this going to last? *How long is he going to be keeping me in the dark? This is almost like Doug. I have met the kids but I am still like this dirty little secret. I want to be supportive of William and understanding but I'm not going to allow him to keep me dangling on a string. I have my own issues that I need to deal with but how can I tell him if I am not sure what we are doing?*

Charlice lays her head on William's shoulder and they sit back and talk about work and any other topic that keeps them from talking about the elephant in the room...Karen.

***

"Oh my GOD!" Peaches screams.

While trying to plan for the Girls Trip cruise, Peaches still has to deal with the aftermath of the gala shooting. The shooting almost ruined Peaches' reputation but you know Peaches. She also has something up her sleeve for a great comeback. But the reports and news media have to be dealt with first.

Thanks to her connections in the city and of course the mayor, she was able to work some magic and put out lots of fires and lawsuits. She had to call in some favors and she owes some people some favors.

Thank goodness no one died that night. It was a miracle that Jaime's husband survived the eight gunshots.

Peaches reaches out to Jaime to make sure that Jamie is still going to join the getaway with the ladies. "Hey Jamie! How are you doing?"

"Hi Peaches! Everything is going great. I am just getting myself ready for this Girls Trip Cruise. I am so excited. You know I need a good girl's getaway."

"I know that's right. You need this trip more than anyone I know." Peaches agrees.

Jamie starts, "Yah, Maurice decided that we should go our separate ways because he is going to jail for shooting my husband. He felt like I brought way too much drama in his life. He has to think about his future after jail. Even though he made the decision to shoot my husband, I bring too much drama to his life."

"Wow!" Peaches exclaims. "How do you feel about that?"

"I am a little hurt by his decision but I understand. He knows that I am not going to stick around and wait for him or so he believes. I think he needs to count his blessings that my husband did not die. He says that I didn't truly understand all that he endured in the relationship with me. Like the verbal abuse from my husband. He said the final straw was my husband's actions at the party. He snapped."

"Well maybe I can talk to some people and try to work on getting that sentence reduced. If he truly endured some bullying from your husband, perhaps he doesn't deserve such a harsh sentence. I will look into it." This was part of Peaches' plan. Make the husband who got shot look like the aggressor and make it look like he may have deserved to be shot. "No matter what, you need this 14-day adventure with the girls. Who is going to take care of the kids?"

"My aunt is going to watch my children. It is their spring break from school so they will have one week at home with my mother and one week with their father's sister."

"Perfect! I will see you in a few weeks ready for an unforgettable experience. Bye Jamie!"

Peaches needs this getaway too. So much has happened. She bears the weight of the city on her shoulders. She feels overwhelmed but doesn't like to show weakness.

Peaches' phone beeps with a notification from Superman.

It's a text message. The message reads: *The Winston suite #2014 ASAP.*

She smiles. Then sends a heart eyes emoji along with the message: *1 hour.*

Peaches freshens up, gets dressed, grabs her purse, looks in the mirror, smiles. *Meeting at The Winston.* Then heads out the door.

***

Peaches pulls up to the front of The Winston. She is met by a handsome young tall brown skinned valet. He opens her car door and reaches for her hand. "Good Afternoon Miss Peaches! Mr. Anderson has left this for you." The young valet hands her a key card.

"Why thank you young man." Peaches steps out of the car and makes the necessary adjustments to her dress and hair.

"Enjoy your stay at The Winston." The young man winks his left eye and gently slides into the driver's seat of her car. Then drives off.

Peaches walks through the hotel lobby trying not to think about the last time that she was there. She looks over to her right and sees the corner that Karen was balled up in. *Poor Karen.* Peaches thinks but shakes it off and just stays focused on the task at hand. Meeting Mayor Anderson. She notices one of his bodyguards in the lobby. Their eyes meet. The bodyguard gives her a head nod and she offers him a smile.

Peaches enters the elevator and heads up to the 20th floor. The top floor. The doors open and she sees another bodyguard. This one just looks in the opposite direction. Peaches chalks that up to him trying to be discreet since there were some other guests on the floor.

Peaches finds suite 2014 and places the keycard in the door. When she steps into the room, she can hear Jazz music playing softly in the background. The suite has a small sitting room when you first walk in the door. Kent is not in the seating area. Peaches takes her pumps off at the door and lays her handbag and key card down on the table in the foyer.

"Is that you Miss Peaches?" A deep dark voice says from around the corner of the suite.

Peaches closes her eyes and smiles. *Ooohhh!* How she loves to hear that man call her name. His deep dark sexy voice just makes her melt inside. Like an episode of The Dating Game, she peeps around the corner to see the face that matches that sexy ass voice.

There sitting up on the bed with his ankles crossed and his laptop on a bed tray is Kent wearing only his black boxer briefs. Peaches stands there for a moment just to take in all that she sees, the muscles and the tight abs and especially that huge bulge in the black boxer briefs.

Kent looks up. "Good Afternoon Miss Peaches. It is so nice

of you to finally accept my invitation for a meeting. Due to unforeseen circumstances we were unable to have our scheduled meeting at this same location at the originally scheduled day and time."

"Of course, Mr. Mayor. I serve at your pleasure." Peaches starts to unbuckle her dress as she needs to get appropriately dressed for her meeting with the mayor. "I do apologize for the inconvenience. I know that you are an extremely busy man and I understand that your time is precious." She lets her dress drop to the floor. "But here I am. Ready for my debriefing. Now can I get you anything before we start the meeting? Coffee? Tea? Fruit?"

Kent closes his laptop and moves the table out of his way so that he can get a better look at Peaches standing there in nothing but a lacy crimson red bra and a matching crimson red thong. She knew his favorite color. It was the little things that Peaches did that drew him to her; that made him want her so badly every time he saw her and every time he thought about her. As he stood up on his two feet, the bulge in his briefs stood up as well. He walks towards her. "Miss Peaches, I am ready for my taste." He pulls her into his body and slowly glides the bulge across her hip and thigh.

Peaches smiled as she felt the pulsating bulge on her leg. She knew exactly what that meant. She knew exactly what he wanted from her. She releases the bulge into her soft hands and begins to caress every inch of it over and over again.

She tilts her head to the side and Kent begins to gently kiss her neck. The gentle kisses on the neck quickly turn into sucks on the neck, shoulder and breasts. Then intensify into nibbles on her flesh. Peaches does not resist. She accepts every kiss and every nibble with moans of pleasure. Kent grabs one of Peaches' ears with his lips and whispers, "You like that, huh?"

"Ooohh! Yes! You know I do." Peaches responds between kisses and moans.

"I am ready for my taste. Are you ready, Miss Peaches?" Kent asks.

"Yes, daddy! I am ready." Peaches moans.

Kent moves Peaches back towards the bed and then slams her face down on the side of the bed. He stands behind and admires the view. There she is lying face down bent over with her arms above her head. This is how he likes Peaches. He rubs the sides of her hips. Then places one of his legs between her legs to make room for him to slide his manhood inside of her. Over and over he inserts himself inside of her. Harder, harder. Then faster and faster as Peaches' moans and his thrusts sync together in rhythm.

He then places Peaches up on the bed and on her back. He puts her legs up in the air and opens them wide. Peaches looks up at Kent and says, "Have a taste." Kent smiles and starts kissing, sucking, licking and nibbling between Peaches legs the same way he had treated the rest of her body at the beginning of the meeting. Peaches screams in absolute uncontrollable pleasure.

When Kent comes up to give Peaches a break, Peaches tackles him, rolling him on his back and she hops on top for her ride. As Peaches sits on top of Kent, he begins to moan with pleasure. For the next hour or so, Peaches and Kent go roll around in the bed making love. No interruptions, just the two of them for that moment in time.

When they have finished, they lay there in the bed holding each other. Peaches knows this is the perfect time to ask him for anything that she needs. "Kent, you were amazing. I have missed you so much. You always know exactly what I need when I need it. I needed you that night of The Ivory Soiree but you know what happened." She kisses him on the chest.

Kent pulls Peaches tighter to his chest. "I am so sorry about your event. I have my people working on the cleanup. I told them to make sure that this does not have any effect on your reputation, or the organization or the hotel. They are working on it. I promise. I will not let anything happen to you. You know you can count on me."

"Thank you so much Kent. You truly are my Superman. But I do need to ask for your help regarding the incident."

"What do you need? I will get my people on it." Kent sits up eager to come to Peaches' rescue.

"So the guy who actually did the shooting really doesn't

deserve to go to jail or prison. He's a good guy."

"What? But he shot someone eight times in front of your gala. His actions almost ruined your business and ruined me for attending a so-called ghetto affair. Do you know what they are calling your event? The Ivory Soiree Massacre. Even though the guy didn't die, socially and politically, this could be a massacre to our careers. But now you want me to defend this guy's actions? Please explain."

Peaches pleads, "Kent, I know what you are saying but look at the bigger picture. The guy who got shot was abusive. He had threatened the guy who shot him. He was a bully. He was a horrible person. Defending him would political suicide. Please Kent. Use your power to help him."

"Okay Peaches. I will look into it. Perhaps we can make this issue fade away. You and I will just keep doing what we are doing. We will let our Public Relations people fix the issues. Agreed?"

"Thank you my Superman." Peaches smiles. "I knew you could help me." Peaches lay on Kent's chest content…

Kent and Peaches lay in the bed talking and laughing for another hour or so until they realize that they both need to go. Kent needs to get home to his wife and Peaches off to plan her Vision Board Party and her Girls Excursion Cruise.

Peaches thinks as she looks in the mirror to fix her makeup, *yes all it took was some great sex and I got my way. Kent will fix this.* They kiss and part ways until the next time.

"You are the gatekeeper to your life and your home. You get to decide who or what comes in and what needs to stay out. If it doesn't contribute to the peaceful home you are now trying to have, then it should stay out." — Jen Grice, You Can Survive Divorce: Hope, Healing, and Encouragement for Your Journey

Chapter X: *The Forewarn Blame*

Fault Advancement

All William wanted was to live his life now. Live a happy life. He saw the signs and the red flags with Karen but he felt obligated because of Karen's history.

William goes over to visit his best friend John. He hadn't been back to John's house since he moved out. "I miss you John. I miss being your roommate, man."

John smirks, "No you don't. You enjoy being in your own space. You enjoy having your kids over and you enjoy having Charlice laid up under you."

William laughs, "You're right. I enjoy my own space and damn sure don't enjoy coming into your home and one week there will be some man in here and the next week a woman. Sometimes I was just as confused as you are."

"Shut up, Man. You're stupid." John laughs.

"John, we have come such a long way. When you and I lived in that group home, who would have imagined our lives being like this?"

172

John shakes his head. "I'm sure people expected us to be dead, in the streets or in jail. We beat those odds didn't we? Both of us are successful businessmen. You have your beautiful family. We have truly been blessed."

"We sure did. When are you going to settle down and have a family?"

"With my lifestyle, do you really think I am going to have a family?" John laughs. "No sir, that is not the life for me. I like how I live. I am attracted to people and the way someone makes me feel. I look at people as individuals. Gender is not important to me. I love who I love. I would never bring a new life into the mix of my lifestyle. My child would be so confused. Plus, I don't see myself committing myself to just one person for the rest of my life. That is the life that you have chosen. So how is Karen? How are the kids?"

William is silent and shakes his head just thinking about all of the drama that he has endured these past few weeks. "Karen is Karen. She hasn't changed. No matter how many times I have told her about my concerns. No matter how much I support her. No matter how many times I have begged her to change…She is still Karen. The children are adjusting well to living in two separate homes. Will J just wants to be a kid. On the other hand, Willow wants to know why. She even asked me about Charlice the other day. I wasn't prepared to answer her questions."

"Friend, you are going to have to answer her sooner or

later. What are you going to tell her? What are you doing with Charlice?"

"Charlice is the one. She is a breath of fresh air. I smile when I am around her. She is independent. She doesn't rely on me for everything. Everything that I give her and everything I do for her is just because. It isn't because I have to do it. It is because she appreciates it and because it makes both of us happy. She doesn't demand things like Karen. I want to marry her John."

"But Will, you are married to Karen. You pledged yourself to Karen almost 20 years ago. You can't turn your back on your marriage. Did you really try to make it work? I remember you telling me 20 years ago that Karen was the one. Do you remember that?"

"I have tried. You know I have tried. I tried even after Will J was born. I even tried while we were separated. I asked her to go to counseling. And now all of a sudden she wants to go. It's almost like she senses that I am done. I bought this house for the kids and I. Charlice has moved in. I am ready to restart my life without her."

"But wait a minute. What did you tell the kids about Charlice? Have they met her?"

"Yes, the kids met my friend Miss Charlice. Willow has the questions. She wants to know if that is my new girlfriend. She's a smart girl. I am going to tell her all about Charlice. I am going to tell her about my plans to divorce Karen."

"Whoa!" John stands up. "Are you sure about this? Karen wants to do counseling now. I think you should go?"

William with tears in his eyes, "John, I am tired. I want to move on. I want to start to heal from this relationship. Charlice can help me do that. I am ready. I know I am. I have been considering this for a long time. Even when I was staying here with you, I was thinking about this. I didn't plan on meeting and falling in love with Charlice. My marriage will not work unless Karen gets counseling for herself."

"Hear me out Will." John sits down close to his friend. "Think about how we grew up. We basically raised ourselves. We didn't have the benefit of having active parents. We vowed that we would never let our children endure any type of pain when it came to their home lives. As your friend, I am begging you; please give counseling a try. If not to save your marriage, then to save your children from some of the pain that we felt."

William sits silently looking at his friend.

"I urge you Will just try to make your family work before you move on. It is better if you try to get some closure to this relationship. You have to make sure your feelings are gone before you move on to the next one. It wouldn't be fair to Charlice if you harbor any lingering feelings."

William puts his head down and thinks about everything his friend is saying. I really feel like Karen only wants to make us work so she can keep up the appearance of a happy perfect family. How would it look to her bougie friends if her marriage fell apart and she was lying and describing this perfect life. Karen will lose her mind if her perfect little family falls apart. Can I really go back to Karen after the happiness that I have been experiencing with Charlice?

"John, I have heard everything that you said. I will consider everything that we talked about. I will keep you updated on my decision. Thank you friend." William stands up and hugs John.

"Anytime friend. Love you."

"I will see you later. I need to go talk to my family."

Driving in his Jeep, William is rethinking about his conversation with John. *My marriage with Karen was great at the beginning but things have changed. I'm just not happy with Karen anymore. I love my children and I want to be there for them but if I am not happy I cannot make my children happy. We will all die inside. What my children see now will affect them as adults.*

William makes his decision. He calls Karen. "Hey Karen! We need to talk. I thought about counseling. And I don't think it is a good idea. I think it is time that we go our separate ways."

Karen is flabbergasted. "Go our separate ways? What do you mean? What about our family? How could you say such a thing? How could you even think like that?

176

What about the children?"

William stops her. "Karen, this is for the children. This is for me and this is for you. None of us has been happy for the past few years. I'm tired Karen. You have never respected me nor have you ever appreciated me as a man. You have always treated me like I was an accessory."

Karen cannot hold back her tears. "I will admit it. I did not know who to treat you. I really didn't know about relationships because of what I went through." She breaks down sobbing and tries to make William feel bad. "You knew my story; you knew my pain and you still chose to be with me and have a family. You said that you would support me."

William yells back at Karen. "And I have been there for you through thick and thin. I'm not happy and that's the bottom line. I am drowning Karen. I am drowning." He pauses for a moment to catch his breath. "You said that you would get help and seek therapy. You never did. Was I supposed to sit and watch you get worse? Why should I have to keep suffering because you did not want to get help. How dare you do this to me and our children."

"All you think about is yourself. You really only care about your feelings. You only think about yourself. I told you that I found a doctor that could help me. the family and our marriage.

Can we go to Dr. Wells the counselor? Can you give us a chance? William, I am begging you."

"No, why now? Because you know I am serious about moving on with my life. Karen, I want to be happy; I need to be happy. We only have one life to live. Why would I spend my life with a woman who cares nothing about her man and the family?"

"Well it seems like you have made up your mind William. But you know me, I do not give up that easily. I am not a quitter. Just watch William. See what happens." Karen ends the call and throws her phone across the room.

She begins walking up and down the kitchen. "How can he do this to us? William, why would you do this? I told you that I have a marriage and family counselor for us. I told you that I would do better. I hear what you are saying. You want me to change. Okay! I will change." Calming herself down. "Let me start by going to the salon to change my hair. Yes, I will change my hairstyle. I am sure you will like it Dear." Karen heads upstairs to get dressed to go to the salon to tell them all about the spa and the gala.

***

After Karen hangs up on William, he calls Charlice to tell her everything that just happened. He shared the details of his conversation with John. And how John begged him to work things out with Karen. Then he shares with her the conversation with Karen and how he tells Karen it is over

178

and they should go their separate ways. He tells Charlice about how Karen reacted.

William felt like a weight had been lifted off his chest. He had finally told Karen that he was leaving her and that he was done. He could finally start his life with Charlice. He told her how he would talk to the kids about her and how the four of them could live together in the house. William was elated. On the other hand, Charlice was not feeling it.

Charlice doesn't know how to feel at this point. She is confused. Is she going back in time and repeating her same situation with Doug? Is she willing to take a chance on William? Maybe she should have just planted her feet with Guy. There was no serious baggage with Guy. She could have lived her best life with Guy. Why is she really with William? He doesn't even have a divorce yet. Like Doug. Did they even talk about him getting a divorce? What if he doesn't get a divorce? What are her plans? Forget about his plans. Charlice really needed to start thinking about herself. Now she feels like she didn't give herself enough time to heal from Doug. Why didn't she give herself the time she needed to heal? William is talking about himself healing? Should she talk to William about taking some time to heal? This way she could give William time to figure out what he wants to do regarding his family.

At this point, Charlice is so tired of hearing about William and his family. She has concerns of her own that she needs to deal with. *William is so caught up in his family that he doesn't see me and my feelings. I don't know how much more I can take of this.* "William, I will give you a call later. I have a client right now." Charlice hangs up the phone.

That is the second woman to hang up on me today. William decides that he is going to talk to Will J and Willow about his decision.

***

Meanwhile, at the salon…

"Oopp! Here she come y'all. Here she come! Here come Kur'n. Here come Kur'n." Sam is running around jumping up and down. He is so excited to see Karen coming through the door. "All my life…I've been waiting for this moment." Sam musters up some fake tears using his Madea voice.

Everybody in the shop is laughing at him. "You so crazy Sam." Someone shouts out.

Mrs. Karen Lime comes sashaying into the salon. She is wearing blue jeans and a white t-shirt with her Louis Vuitton bag on her left forearm, a Louis Vuitton baseball cap and a huge pair of Louis Vuitton shades. Looking like she is a celebrity incognito. "Hello everyone! It feels like I haven't been here in ages." Karen walks past the receptionist and immediately sashays over to Lou and gives her a big hug and a kiss on each cheek.

"Karen, I haven't seen you in a month of Sundays. How are you?" Lou is happy to see Karen. Lou was really worried about her especially after hearing all of the reports.

"I am fabulous, girl. My wonderful hubby sent me to the spa for some much needed rest and relaxation after the soiree. So now look at my hair." Karen whips her baseball cap off. "Just look at it. It is a mess."

Lou runs her fingers through Karen's hair. "Oooh chile! We are going to have to do something about this. We are going to have to do some deep conditioning and a crotchet just to stretch the hair and give it a break."

"You are in charge Lou."

"Go to the back and get your hair washed by my shampoo girl. Tell her Lou said you need a deep conditioner."

Karen happily heads to the back speaking and waving at everyone she sees. "Hey Sam! How are you?" She goes in to hug him.

"Hey Kur'n! How are you?" He offers her a side hug and air kiss. He is working on a client's hair.

Karen comes back through the shop with her wet hair tied up in a towel. She checks the mirror to make sure her makeup is intact. Then she flops down in Lou's chair.

"Karen, you must have been going through it," Lou looks over at Sam and winks. "because you have not been here in a while."

"I know. I know. I was just so drained after the soiree. You know the planner, Peaches, is a really good friend of mine so I had been helping her with that event. Now she has two events coming up so I have been helping her with those."

"Oh what events does she have planned now?" Lou asks.

"We are planning a Vision Board Party and an All Girls Cruise. After the success of the Ivory Soiree, we just had to immediately start planning for these events. The people want more."

Lou and Sam make eye contact. Sam turns away and busts out laughing. "Lord Jesus take the wheel." Sam screams, shaking his head and looking back down at his client's head. Then says a quick prayer. "Lordt, I pray to you to please, please, please look over your churn'. As some of themma do not know what they sayeth. Please help themma speak the truef. Um shamma lamma shum! In Jesus' namma, we pray. Amen. Amen. Amen.

The clients are laughing but they are confused. Lou bursts out in a full laughter. Karen, oblivious laughs as well.

"Sam, you are so crazy." Lou turns to Karen. "Really Karen? The Soiree was successful. Do tell. I want to hear all about this successful soiree."

Lou had heard all of the stories about the soiree. Everyone in D.C. had heard about the shooting at the event. Now here Karen is saying that it was a success. Lou had to hear this story in detail. Everyone in the shop was anxious to hear what Karen had to say.

"Well, it was in the gorgeous ballroom at The Winston Hotel. The Who's Who of D.C. were there. Mayor Anderson and his wife, judges, senators, congressmen, important business people. I tried to get hubby to go but he wanted to stay home with the kids."

Lou thought, *He wanted to stay home with Charlice is what you mean.*

"There were two Go-Go bands that played. The DJ played music from various genres. We collected over $500,000 for the non-profit organization. We danced all night. We ate. We drank. We socialized. It was wonderful. I got so many compliments on my hair, my makeup and outfit. People will be talking about that party for years." Karen's face lit up with excitement.

Sam mumbles under his breath. "Yep! We will be talking about that party for about 5-10 more years."

Lou cuts her eyes over at Sam, "So there weren't any fights, or arguments? There wasn't any drama?"

Karen sits up almost as if she were offended. "Absolutely not! Not at such a prestigious event as The Ivory Soiree. Peaches would never have allowed that type of riff raff in her party. She would not allow any interlopers to cause such chaos and confusion."

Lou and Sam look at each other again noticing her agitation. Sam asks, "You good Kur'n? Ain't nobody trying to upset you. Lou is just asking questions. Remember us minions were not at the Who's Who Soiree?"

"I am okay Sam. I'm just tired. Or rather I am just relaxed from my time at the spa."

"Oh yes! Tell us all about that Karen." Lou insists.

"Well hubby arranged for me to spend a few days at a spa in Virginia. It was wonderful. I received a facial and a massage. I sat in the sauna." Then she whispered. "Then I had my vagina steamed. Have you had that done Lou?"

"No, I have not tried that before. I have heard some good things about it though."

"You would love it. You sit on this open stool; it's almost like a toilet. Then sit on the pot with your legs to the side. They put a big towel across your lap and the steam rises up into your vagina. It is so invigorating. You can feel the warmth all throughout your body. One of the benefits is that it increases fertility. William told me that he wants to have another child. He insisted that I get them steam so that it would help us conceive sooner. He thinks that a new baby would help us get closer."

"Really? I will have to go get my vagina steamed one day. Not for fertility reasons though. Just as a deep cleanse. Has he found a new house for you all to move into?" Lou knows the answer to that question. She knows that he has already moved into a new house and that Charlice basically lives with him.

"No! He is still looking for the perfect house. If you don't mind me saying, your friend Chartice isn't very good at her job. She is taking so long finding us a home. I'm going to have to find a real estate agent if she doesn't step it up. William doesn't want to tell her. He wants me to tell her."

Lou gets defensive. "CharLICE is a terrific realtor. Perhaps your husband is the issue. Maybe you should talk to him again. Maybe he is the one who doesn't know what he really wants or maybe he just wants too much."

"Sorry Lou. I didn't mean to upset you. Charlice, Is that her name? Is your friend but she's just not doing her job to MY satisfaction."

"Look Karen, I am not going to allow you to speak negatively about my friend. All of your concerns need to be addressed to YOUR husband. He has all of the answers. And that is all that I am going to say about that."

For the rest of the time that Karen is in Lou's chair, she rambles on and on about the vision board party, the all girls cruise, her marriage and her wonderful life.

Lou gives her short answers and just answers with "Yes" or "No" when appropriate. No matter how much she disagrees with Charlice's decisions sometimes, that is still her girl, her best-friend, her sister-friend. Lou cannot wait to talk to Charlice and tell her what Karen said in the shop.

Karen calls William to let him know that she is almost finished and that he needs to come pay for her hair. About

15 minutes later William arrives to pay Lou for Karen's hair.

When William walks in the shop, he greets everyone with a smile and daps up Sam. Lou rolls her eyes and just looks at him like he is crazy. William is taken aback by her behavior but just brushes it off.

Lou decides to speak up, "Hey William! Karen was just updating us on your house hunt. She said that you all haven't been able to locate a house for your family and that you might be looking for a new real estate agent."

William looks at Lou. He now understands the reason behind her giving him the cold shoulder. After all, she is Charlice's best friend. "Well Lou, as you already know, these things take time. Sensitive issues need to be dealt with before moving forward. As I am sure that Charlice has explained to you."

Lou knows what William means but she just wanted some clarification. As Charlice's best friend and as Karen's stylist, she is in the middle of two different stories. On the one hand, Charlice is telling her that she and William are in love. He is leaving Karen. She has met the kids and they are about to be one big happy family in their new home. On the other hand, she has Karen painting this beautiful picture of her family. Her loving husband and beautiful children are searching for their perfect forever home. Not to mention the fact that William comes in here every time Karen gets her hair done and pays for it. *Why can't he just Zelle her*

186

the money or give her a debit card? This entire dynamic is odd. I do not know why Charlice would want to get caught up in this mix.

William walks over to Karen, "I love your hair. I am leaving now. I have some things that I need to take care of. The kids and I will stop by Sunday so we can see if you are ready for them to come home. I will also check in with your doctor to see what she says."

"Doctor?" Lou asks. "You didn't mention anything about going to a doctor. Is everything okay with you? Are you feeling okay?"

Karen laughs it off. "Yes! Yes! Everything is fine. William just worries about me. That is why he sent me to the spa. Isn't that right Dear?'

William looks at Karen. Tilts his head to the side. "Lou, and everyone else enjoy the rest of your day. Karen…we will talk Sunday." He walks out of the salon.

Lou removes the smock from across Karen's body and lowers her chair. "Okay Karen! You are all set. Will you be in next week?"

"Oh Yes! I will be here Tuesday and then Thursday. I want to get back to my regular routine." Karen stands up and reaches in her bag. She puts her shades on. Places her handbag on her left forearm and sashays back out of the shop. Waving goodbye like a queen as she walks out.

187

Sam imitates her walk through the salon and swings his imaginary hair. "I am Karen Lime." He says in a high pitched snooty voice. "And I am better than all of you bitches in here because my life is perfect. My husband has a girlfriend and I spent a week in the hospital strapped down."

"Stop Sam." Lou smacks his arm. "We don't know that."

"Yes we do. You can act like you don't know. You can act as crazy as she is but we all know the truth." Sam stops working on his client's hair to get serious. "Again, you better tell Charlice to be careful. She needs to be really careful. You see how William wouldn't back up what she said. She lives in her own little perfect world." He thinks. " I wonder if she hears crazy music in her head. You know like in those scary movies when the crazy person hears music like La la la! La la la! La la la la la la la!"

Everybody in the shop is laughing at Sam and dissecting Karen's story. Lou is quiet.

Lou does worry about Charlice and William and Karen. That is a scary love triangle. Lou has her own concerns though. *Charlice is grown. Plus, you can't tell her anything. She will learn one day. What happens in the dark always comes to the light. Karen is going to find out about the affair. And I will be right here listening to both sides.* Lou laughs and joins in the conversation. Patiently waiting for her next client to arrive.

"The search for a scapegoat is the easiest of all hunting expeditions." — Dwight D. Eisenhower

Chapter XI: *The Designed Entrance*

"Planned Passage"

Sunday afternoon William and the children pull up to the Tinsley house. The atmosphere is a little off. The three of them look at each other because each one of them is feeling it.

The house is dark but Karen's Range Rover is in the garage.

Will J calls out for his mother. "Mom, we are home."

They all hear a moan coming from upstairs. William tells the kids to stay down here. "Let me make sure your mom is okay." He sprints up the stairs into Karen's room.

He finds her lying flat on her back across the bed disheveled as if she had just gotten into a fight and lost. "Karen, are you okay? He hesitates to go over to her but he decides to approach her slowly.

"NO!" Karen lifts her head up and screams. "No I am not. My life is falling apart. William please, please, please move back in with me. I need you. I will do anything that you ask me to do. I can fix this. WE can fix this. I am begging you.

190

I asked you to go to counseling with me and you told me no." Karen lays her head back down and cries in silence contemplating her life and the changes that may occur. *How will I maintain my lifestyle? Will he continue to give me the amount of money I want to continue to live the lifestyle I have been living all of these years?*

William is frustrated. "Karen, for years, I told you that I was unhappy and for years I begged you to get help but you ignored my request. You left me no choice but to leave."

He takes a deep breath and starts to break it down about why they can no longer be together. He has been damaged by her mistakes. "Here I am a prestigious, DMV accountant with some millionaire clients and my name is on the foreclosure list and I was in the process of filing bankruptcy because my wife has a shopping addiction and wants to keep up with the Jones.' Do you have any idea how many clients your antics cost me? Do you know how challenging it has been for me to rebuild my reputation in the DC community? That is why I have chosen to move to Largo. I have to get out of DC. You say that I do not care about you. When have you shown any care or consideration to me Karen? I cannot try to be happy with someone who does not understand that they are the problem. I cannot be with you if you do not seek the mental health support that you need."

Karen sits up straight after listening to William. "Well maybe I should just go away or maybe I should just end my life now. Who is going to care if I die?" Karen puts her

191

head in her hands but at the same time she is peeking through her fingers watching William's reaction.

William is standing next to the bed rolling his eyes at her dramatics and the fact that she really did not hear what he said. He has seen it all before. He has fallen for it so many times but he is over it now. He asks, "Are you finished now Karen?"

Karen looks up at him. "You don't care if I kill myself do you? You don't care that I am feeling depressed and suicidal."

"If that is how you feel Karen, then go see your psychiatrist. You are the main one who needs to go to counseling for yourself. God helps those who help themselves first."

"Okay William. I understand. I am telling you that I am feeling suicidal and you don't care. You aren't listening to me. I have a plan, you know." Karen knows she cannot survive without William.

"Okay Karen. What is your plan? Please share it with me." William folds his arms; he is dying to hear her plan; he does not believe her.

"I am going to get some OxyContin or something. Then I am going to get all dressed up in my sexiest evening gown. I am going to make up my face and fix my hair nice and pretty. Then I am going to eat my favorite meal. Next I am going to take the entire bottle of pills. Then finally I am going to lay down and never wake up again. I won't leave a note because you already know the why. Make sure the children don't find me first. You can find me and then tell them how you were responsible for Mommy's death. Watch me William. Then all of your problems will be solved. No more Karen. You would like that huh? Wouldn't you, William?"

William looks at his wife. Smiles. Shakes his head. Then walks out of the room and closes the door. Everything that he was thinking about Karen turns out to be true. She is mentally unstable. She needs help. The kids want to sleep in their own beds and go to school from their house. He is hesitant about allowing them to stay with Karen overnight but he concedes to their request. *You know what...she just wants my attention. She is fine. The kids will be okay tonight. I will check on them tomorrow.*

William knows that Karen loves her children too much to harm herself just because he wants to move on with his life and be happy with Charlice, so he believes. He remembers his conversation with John and thinks about putting the relationship to rest with a counseling session. *Maybe if I got to counseling, the counselor will tell us that we need to go our separate ways.*

On his way home, William decides to call Charlice. He wants to be honest with Charlice in everything but he knows that is not possible. He loves Charlice but to be honest with himself, he doesn't know her that well to share everything. *I hope Charlice is patient enough to*

193

understand all of my baggage.

On the phone, William cautiously tells Charlice all about his encounter with Karen and how Karen threatened to kill herself. "She has never done that before. Today she gave me an entire plan. She wants us to go to counseling as a couple. John thinks that maybe we should so that the counselor could support me in moving on."

Charlice is in aww. She doesn't know what to say. *What if Karen is crazy enough to kill herself? He hasn't even told Karen about her yet. That just might be the one thing to send her over the edge. I don't want to be one of the causes of this woman's death. Plus, William is clearly concerned even though he won't admit it.* "William, perhaps you should go to counseling. Just to say you tried. If not, for the children, then for yourself."

"I've tried to work things out with her Charlice. I have really tried. But since you and John feel so strongly about me going, I will weigh my options. Thank you for listening to me vent Baby. I don't know what I would do without you. I will be home in about 20 minutes. I will see you then."

After William talks to Charlice, he decides to go to family counseling. Her support is what he needed. He feels like he owes it to his family especially after talking to John, as well. The two most important people in his life think that he should try counseling. "What could family counseling hurt?"

194

***

Charlice starts to have second thoughts about the relationship. Something is not sitting well with her. Her gut tells her so much more but she doesn't know what her gut is trying to tell her. *Should I stick with him and ride the relationship out? Should I wait for him to get his family issues straight? What if he decides to stick with Karen? He is a great man and has been treating me like a queen from the very start. But so did Guy. To be honest, Guy treated me much better especially on the material level and Guy doesn't have any baggage. Did I make a mistake about walking away from Guy? Will I be able to go back if I want to?*

Charlice needed to get some rest. She was overworking her body and mind and needed to slow down. After all, she couldn't only consider herself and her needs anymore. She had someone else to think about.

***

After William leaves, Karen calls Peaches because she knows that Peaches will have a solution to her situation. "Hey Peaches! It's me. How are you?"

"Girl! I am good but what is wrong with you? You sound so somber."

Sniffing to let Peaches know that she had been crying, Karen mumbles. "I'm so depressed, Peaches. My life is falling apart. William still wants to be alone and I want him

195

to come back home with me and the kids. I'm just so sad. I was just thinking that maybe he would prefer for me to die."

"Girl Bye!" Peaches blows off Karen's concerns. "He loves you. You just need to stop playing games with that man. You need to use some of your womanly ways to get that man back. Stop being motherly and start acting like you did when you got him. I know them little girls were chasing his fine chocolate ass back then. You're the one that got him."

Karen and Peaches share a laugh. Then Karen gets serious again.

"You are right. But we are not the same people. I have a plan to get him back but I may need your help friend."

"What do you need from Peaches, friend? You know I am here to help you."

"I need you to get me a large quantity of OxyContin. My plan is to make William think that I am going to commit suicide. I want him or Willow to find me lying unconscious. But in reality I will have taken some Melatonin. My plan is brilliant. Can you help me?"

"Have you lost your ever lovin' mind? You want me to get you some WHAT to make it look like you attempted suicide? Do I have drug dealer written across my forehead?" Peaches is pissed. "William told you that he needed space. He didn't say go kill yourself."

"Peaches, please I need your help. He said he wants to move on. He said he doesn't want to attend counseling. He wants me to move on. My entire lifestyle will change without him."

"Have you considered the fact that William has found someone else? Has that ever crossed your mind? Do you think that he has moved on? Do you…"

"HE WOULD NEVER DO THAT TO ME? HE WOULD NEVER CHEAT ON ME? HE WOULD NEVER VIOLATE OUR WEDDING VOWS?" Karen is screaming at the top of her lungs. "HOW CAN YOU SAY THAT? YOU KNOW HE LOVES ME? YOU'RE SUPPOSED TO BE MY FRIEND PEACHES. YOU DON'T EVEN KNOW WHAT YOU'RE TALKING ABOUT!"

"WHOA Karen! You need to calm down. I am your friend. That's why I am trying to talk to you calmly. If you were another bitch on the street, I would cuss your ass out for disrespecting me. You asked me for help. I am just trying to get you to think about some things." Peaches is pissed. She would really like to roll over to Karen's house and slap the taste out of her mouth but that's what the old Peaches from Berry Farms would have done? Plus, she cannot afford another scandal dealing with a violent act.

"Sorry Peaches. I lost myself for a moment. I am listening to you."

"That's better. You need to go ahead and make that

appointment with Dr. Wells immediately. Don't wait for William to give you a time. That way you are showing him that you have made the effort to work on yourself. Do that before you go through with this elaborate scheme."

Peaches starts to think Karen is truly crazy. *Why would Karen want to kill herself over a man, when she has two beautiful children that need her love and care?* Peaches knows some of Karen's traumas but doesn't think that any of her traumas warrant death.

Peaches thinks *Karen's plan is a very bad idea, but I am willing to help her save her marriage. I have had some crazy friends but I don't have any that fit the bill of Karen. Who in the world, other than Karen, would set up an elaborate plan just to get a man back?*

"Okay Peaches! I will make the appointment with Dr. Wells. I will let you know how our first session goes. Love you! Talk at you later." Karen feels relieved having talked to Peaches.

She immediately calls Dr. Wells' office and sets up an appointment for Friday at 1:00 p.m. She then texts William with the information. William replies back with a thumbs up emoji. Karen is so excited. She cannot wait until Friday. "Dr. Wells will make him come home to me and our family." She smiles to herself.

***

Dr. Suzanne Wells is the best marriage counselor in the

DMV. She has managed to repair almost every dysfunctional marriage that has come through her office.

That Friday Karen arrives early to Dr. Wells' office. That morning she made sure that she got all dressed up in one of her nicest blue day dresses that she purchased from Saks 5th Avenue. She paired that with a pair of navy blue pumps and a simple little navy blue handbag. She decided that she would try a monochromatic look today. This would make her look professional and less flashy even though the cost of her outfit cost a measly $4000.

Karen filled out all of the insurance paperwork and patiently waited for William and Dr. Wells. She looked down at her watch. It was now 1:00pm. *Where is William?* She said to herself. *Oh God! I hope he didn't change his mind.* She searches through her bag and pulls out a compact mirror just to check her makeup. *Perfect!*

Just then a young girl comes through the door leading to the treatment area. She looks over at Karen, smiles and asks, "Mrs. Lime?"

Karen jumps up, "Yes?"

"Dr. Wells is ready for you and your husband. Is Mr. Lime with you?" The young lady asks.

In her usual Karen tone, "Oh yes! William will be here. He is running late completing a business deal. He will be here shortly." Karen had no clue where William was but she couldn't let herself believe that he wasn't going to show up

199

to save their marriage.

Karen follows the young lady into a door. Dr. Well's is sitting in a room that looks like someone's living room. She is sitting in a high back chair with a clipboard in her hand. She stands up when she sees Karen.

"Come in Karen. Is it okay if I call you Karen?"

Karen barely hears what Dr. Wells is saying because she is surprised by the setup of the room. The last time she was in therapy the walls were white and less inviting. This room was warm and cozy. Karen felt like she had just entered the home of Dr. Wells. She shook her head yes to Dr. Wells.

"Thank you, Karen!" Dr. Wells looks towards the door. "Will William be joining us?"

Before Karen could give her rehearsed answer, William comes rushing through the door. "Sorry I am late." He says almost out of breath and reaching his hand out to Dr. Wells. "I had a last minute business meeting that held me up." In reality, he was held up because someone was providing him with some valuable information that could change his life. Plus, he really didn't want to be there anyway.

Dr. Wells invites the Limes to sit down on the sofa. Karen places her hand on top of William's as they sit on the sofa. William slowly pulls his hand away. He wants to make it clear to Karen and the doctor that he does not want to save this marriage.

Dr. Wells starts off the session by asking William and Karen a question. "So William and Karen, why are we here in marriage counseling? What happened to bring us here? What went wrong?" She looks down at her notepad ready to take notes.

"I really do not know why I am here." Said Karen, fighting back her tears. "William moved out of our home about a year ago. He said that he needed space and recently he said he was just tired of me and my ways. I don't even know what I did wrong." She pulls a tissue from the box sitting on the coffee table in front of her. She wipes the tear that has formed in her right eye.

William looks over at Karen with a smirk on his face. "Really? You did not do anything. Dr. Wells, since this session is only 45 minutes, I will give you the bootleg version of what is going on." William sits back and gets comfortable. "For years, I have been telling Karen that I was unhappy. Karen spends money like I have an infinite amount. For example, I bet this outfit that she has on costs about a good $10,000 including the jewelry."

Karen thinks, Dang! *He's right.* I wasn't even considering the jewelry.

"She spends money like this all the time. I am an accountant. I own my company and sometimes I do not have clients. Money is not always consistent. I have explained this to her many times, but she continues to put me into financial binds. We almost lost our house and I

201

almost had to file bankruptcy. I dug us out of several holes.
She isn't supportive. We weren't doing anything together.
She cared more about how people looked at us and how
much other people had. I am tired. I love Karen but my
love is not the same. I want to move forward with my life. I
have done my part. Now I am ready to end this."

Dr. Wells writes down some notes. "I see. So William,
what have you done to save your marriage? Karen, what
have you done to save your marriage? Have you all sought
professional help before today?"

In unison, the Limes reply, "No!"

Dr. Wells laughs, "So what I am hearing is that you two
really did not try hard enough. Before you walk away
William, can you try some of my methods? Karen, are you
willing to try? After all, you two have over 10 years
together and two children."

Immediately, Karen shakes her head yes.

On the other hand, William sits quietly. He looks at Karen.
Then he asks, "Is William Jr. my son?"

In shock, Karen looks at him wide eyed and angry. "I
cannot believe that you would ask me such a thing. Yes he
is yours. Of course, he is your son. What would ever give
you that impression? Where is this coming from?"

In reality, Karen doesn't remember having an affair with
Billy, her ex. Over 10 years ago in their marriage, William

was struggling to make the money that Karen required him to earn to maintain her lifestyle. One day, she ran into Billy while she was shopping. They reconnected and had a brief affair but it ended when Karen realized that Billy had not changed and was only using her for her money and sex. So she broke it off and returned to William. During this time, Karen ended up pregnant but since she blocked the affair out of her mind, William is Will J's father.

"My sources have told me otherwise." says William.

Dr. Wells asks, curiously, "What sources, William?"

"Yeah! What sources?" Karen chimes in angrily.

"I cannot disclose that information. I just can't. Karen knows why. It's because of my clients and the non-disclosure agreements that I have signed. Sharing my source would be unethical. I value the privacy of my clients."

William is a specialized accountant that knows how to hide large amounts of money. He has all types of clients that he has to be extremely secretive about. The DMV is a small area with six degrees of separation between its inhabitants. William has always had his doubts about his son but he has loved William Jr since day one. He is his son.

Karen breaks out into a deep sob. "William, it isn't true. Will J is your son, I know what my faults are. I know that I worry too much about what other people have and that I should be happy with what we have. I know that I should have paid more attention to you and your needs as my husband. But I don't know if I can change at this point but I do know that I am willing to do whatever I need to make our marriage work. I still love you William."

"Okay guys. Let's pause for a moment. From what I can see, there has been a breakdown of communication between the two of you. We need to get back to that. We need to try. We have just scratched the surface and we need to dig deeper. William, are you willing to try? Are you willing to try to improve your communication with Karen?

No matter which way this counseling goes, the communication needs to be better for at least the children. Wouldn't you agree?"

William shakes his head in agreement. William knows that once Karen realizes she can't change, she will then let him go and move on with his life. Perhaps counseling was a good idea after all.

Dr. Wells offers some suggestions that she wants William and Karen to try. "According to marriage expert Edmond Bart, who I model my practice after, Addictions, affairs and excessive anger are relationships' deal-breakers. Bart suggests ending your marriage if your spouse has these three A's. Now we need to have more sessions to see if either of you fall under the three A's but until then let's work on these seven tasks. 1) Share each other's happy moments, 2) Blame the problem, not your spouse 3) Eliminate the three A's that ruin marriages, 4) Kiss each other more, 5) Let your conflict lead to listening, 6) Know the difference between quality and quantity and 7) Ask yourself why you want to make this work. I will print these out for you so that you two can see how you are going to make time to do this and we will work on some of these in counseling. Are you ready to do this?"

Karen is excited. "Yes, I am ready. Let's do it." She looks over at William.

William is silent.

Dr. Wells looks over at William, "William, we are waiting on your answer. Are you ready?"

William shakes his head yes. He knows that he can't follow all of those steps. He knows that he is not going to and he knows that Karen is not going to either. Once Dr. Wells realizes that it isn't going to work, then he will be ready to move on and so will Karen.

"Wonderful!" Dr. Wells exclaims, "We will start off by meeting once a week. I would like to meet the children as well. Initially, I would like to meet them individually. Then meet them together. Then we can all meet together. It looks like we have a lot of work to do to get this family back together. You all know I have a 98% success rate. And I do not give up easily. Now are there any questions?"

Karen is so excited. "I don't have any questions. Do you have any questions, Dear?" She looks over at William smiling.

"No!" William answers, irritated.

"Well that ends our session. William can you stay a moment? I would like to ask you some more questions."

Karen walks out but is very curious about what Dr. Wells wants to talk to her husband about. "Okay Dr. Wells; see you next week. I will go to the receptionist and make the appointment. William, I will see you at home."

Karen walks out and William sits up. "Yes, Dr. Wells? What would you like to discuss?"

"Thank you for staying." Dr. Well puts her notepad down and sits up. "My sources inform me that there may be some other issues that may be affecting the success of your marriage."

"Like what Dr. Wells?" William asks.

"Oh! Like your wife's behavior at The Winston, the night of the shooting. Like you and a beautiful real estate agent. That seems like a huge issue that may be blocking the success of your marriage."

William laughs. "Oooh Dr. Wells! You did some homework on us didn't you?"

"Of course I did." She smirks. "I have to. This IS the DMV, a box. Everybody knows everybody or somebody knows somebody who knows somebody. You know how that goes. I have a lot of highfalutin clients who employ some prestigious accountants. Plus, I know Peaches."

"So Suzanne, do you plan to tell Peaches or Karen about the real estate agent? After all, you said you know about my wife's behavior at The Winston. So you know she is very fragile. She needs therapy. She needs more than marriage counseling."

"I hear you Mr. Lime. I understand. I hear you loud and clear. Like I said during our session, let's work together on these seven steps. Let's work together on getting the family in a better place so that everyone can be happy, not just one person in the family. Can we work together on that, Sir?"

William stands up. "Yes, we can Dr. Wells. I would like that very much." He reaches out his hand to shake hers to seal the deal. "And next week, I will be sure to be on time." He heads towards the door.

"See you next week, William." Suzanne Wells knows everybody in the DMV area. She knows that Karen needs a psychiatrist. She knows that she has taken on a lot with this family but she will help Peaches' friend Karen and Karen's family no matter how many years it takes her. She shakes her head as she laughs out loud. "This is going to be interesting."

***

Karen sat in her truck waiting for William to come out. When she sees him, she calls him over. "Hey Dear! What did Dr. Wells want to talk to you about?"

"Oh Dear! She just wanted to make sure that I was really

going to give this a try. You know Karen. I love you so much and I want our marriage to last forever. I know that we both need to make some changes. We can do this together. Again, I know a newer bigger house is just what we need for our fresh start."

"Yes, Dear! I agree. Can we start our 7 steps with step number 4, Kiss more?" Karen puckers up her lips for a kiss.

The kiss is interrupted by a tap on Karen's truck window. It is William.

"Karen, who are you talking to?" William looks confused.

She bursts out laughing. "You Dear; I was talking to you."

William rolls his eyes. "Oh okay! I will see you next week. I have to go pick up the kids. Enjoy your weekend." He walks away and heads towards his car.

Karen continues, "Let's pick up where we left off…step 4…the kiss." She puckers up her lips.

"He tries to find the exit from himself but there is no door." — *Dejan Stojanovic*

Chapter XII: *The Bleak Plot*

Depressing Scheme

Just in case counseling doesn't work, Karen says, "I need a backup plan."

Karen goes online and searches for ways to keep her husband even if he doesn't want the relationship. She had already researched all of the positive ways. But she needs something desperately drastic to make him stay for good. She needs him to feel so obligated that he would never think of ever leaving again. All these positive vibes and stuff may only be temporary. She knows it won't last for long. She knows Dr. Wells' strategies and methods won't last so she didn't want to put any effort into them.

The kids have to be a part of the plan. William loves our kids and would do anything and everything for them. William Jr will help me, but I'm not sure about Willow. She loves her father too much plus she tells him everything. Willow is growing up so fast. WOW! My baby girl is a teenager. She is now developing her own mind and thoughts. Her rebellious nature is just another stage of teenage life.

Willow is going to make the execution of this plan hard. But Willow loves her and would love to see her family back together.

Karen comes up with a plan to make people think that she is going to go off and kill herself. She decides to start by writing Willow and Will J a letter explaining why she decided to leave them but at the same time she has to make sure that they are okay.

She sits down on her bed and takes out a pen and a sheet of her stationary from her bedside table.

Karen writes,

My Dearest Willow and Will J,

Let me start off by saying that I love you two very much. I love you more than anything in the entire world. Leaving you two is the most difficult decision that I have ever had to make. However, I have prayed about this and I know that this is the best decision. Everything I have done and every decision that I have ever made was to make life better for the two of you. I have tried so hard to be the best mother that I could possibly be but in so many ways, I have failed you both. I have failed myself. Please forgive me for all of my mistakes and all of my faults.

Willow, please take care of your brother and your dad. They are going to need your strength. You are now the female head of the family. I am sorry that I won't be able to watch you grow up into the beautiful young lady that you are going to be.

Will J., Mommy will be with you in spirit. You have your dad and Willow to guide you through the difficult times. Be brave, my son. Continue to grow up and make Mommy proud.

Finally, William, you know why it had to be this way. Please don't feel guilty. I tried to be the wife that you wanted me to be but I could not live up to your perfect wife expectations. I'm sorry that I disappointed you. I love you dear, always. Until we meet again.

Love,

Karen/Mom

Karen sobbed as she wrote the letter. She was experiencing emotional pain and she could no longer bear it and she could not bring herself to get the help she needed. She was in denial about needing help.

She thought for a moment, Could I survive life without my husband? What would life look like without William as her husband? These thoughts crossed her mind as she folded the letter and placed it in an envelope and wrote: To my Family Do NOT Open until I am gone.

Karen puts her pen down and places her letter in the top drawer of her bedside table. She lays back to think about her next move. She decides to call Peaches not about her plan but just to talk about her session with Dr. Wells.

"Hey Karen! What's going on girl?" Peaches sounds so chipper on the phone.

"Nothing much. I was just calling to tell you that William and I met with Dr. Wells today. Thank you so much for the referral."

"No problem. Anytime. Anything for you my friend. I take it that your first session went well?" Peaches asks hesitantly.

"Oh yeah! Yeah!" Karen is ecstatic. "William and I were able to talk some things through. He is going to move back in and we are going to work on our marriage in the house together with the children. He is excited too. He really wants to make us work. He is so wonderful. I just know this is going to work for us."

"Well I am so happy for you. Dr. Wells is good. She has fixed some of the worst marriages in the DMV. I have to run now but I will be seeing you this weekend at my Vision Party, correct?"

"Yes, Peaches. I will be there. See you then. Bye!" Karen ends the call.

"Oh my GOD!" Peaches screams. She is now tired of hearing about William all the time. She has been hearing rumors about him being seen with some light-skinned woman. *I don't want Karen to be made a fool of.*

"I need to investigate Charlice. I need to find out who this Charlice is."

Peaches knows of the shop that Lou's manages. She knows that Charlice gets her hair done there. She is friends with Lou. Again DC is small so she starts to ask around. She can ask some of her sources.

"Ah Ha! I have the perfect source." *DC is way too small.* Peaches thinks to herself.

Peaches thinks *I need to connect with my cousin. She is in the real estate game. They all know each other and operate like crabs in the bucket. Real estate is such a dirty game. She will know if anybody would. I haven't spoken to her in a while. She may find it to be a bit shady if I called or texted her out of the blue.*

Peaches thinks out her plan some more. *Maybe, I should*

tell her I am looking for a house or another condo. Will that work? I really got to think long and hard about how I am going to get this info. I do not want to hear my aunt's mouth about using family for resources but never come around any other time. Or I only come around when I want something.

"You know what…they always calling me when one of the little kids is having a fundraiser. Shoot! I can call when I need some information about purchasing a new property."

Peaches calls her cousin. "Hey cousin! This is Peaches. Your cousin. How are you doing?"

Peaches' cousin Lolo pauses for a second, shocked that her bougie cousin Peaches is calling her. "Hey girl. I haven't spoken to you nor have I seen you in person in a month of Sundays. Everything good? I saw you on the news. The shooting at your event. So sorry about that." Peaches' cousin really wasn't sorry. Peaches forgot where she came from. So for Peaches to be dragged through the mud a bit did not bother her at all.

"Yes! It was such an unfortunate incident that could have ruined the entire night but it didn't. Thank goodness the man who got shot survived and no one else was injured. Look at God!" Peaches laughs.

Peaches' Cousin Lolo laughs as well. "So what's up Peaches? How can I help you today?"

"Well, I am looking for a new forever home in the area and

I thought to myself, 'Hum who do I know in the real estate game?' And I thought of you, my Cousin Lolo."

Lolo laughs, "Aww! You thought of me." Lolo answers sarcastically and rolls her eyes. "That is so sweet of you but I do not sell properties. I am a mere receptionist at a real estate agency."

"You are a receptionist at a prestigious real estate agency. You have worked there for years. Stop playing girl. I know you know the ends and outs of real estate. I know you know the top realtors in the DMV. You have been in this game for way too long not to have learned something."

"You are right Peaches. I have learned a little something something about real estate. So are you looking for a house or condo to buy? I know quite a few real estate agents in the area. Just let me know your price range and what you are looking for. I can put you on." Lolo eases up on Peaches a little bit. She knows that having Peaches as a cousin can benefit her as well.

Peaches can tell that Lolo has relaxed her little attitude a bit so she decides to ask. "Well I have friends, William and Karen Lime. They were telling me about this real estate agent that they just loved. I believe her name is something like Charmoose, Chartice, Charlene, Char... something. Anyway, they just love her and recommended her to me. Do you all have a real estate directory so that I can locate her?"

"OMG!" Lolo screams, "I know him. I've seen his fine ass. I thought he bought a house from CharLICE. Charlice Rice. She works in my office. I thought she helped William purchase a house in Upper Marlboro. Maybe he wants two houses. Who knows?"

Jackpot! Peaches thinks. "Wonderful! What do you know about her? Do you have contact information for her?"

"I really don't know that much about her. She seems like good people. She just moved here from Chicago. She was supposed to come to DC earlier but something happened to her so she moved down a few months later. She came highly recommended so Mr. Johnson insisted that we keep her office ready for when she did arrive. I will text you her information so you can contact her yourself."

"Oh! Thank you so much Lori. I will give her a call today. See I knew who to call."

"No problem. Let me know if you need anything else."

"Love you girl." Peaches ends the call. "Great! Now let me get to the bottom of this."

She calls a Private Investigator friend of hers who used to work for the CIA. She asks him to investigate Charlice. "I want to know about her past and her present. Find out everything about this woman." *Let's put an end to these rumors.*

***

Karen arrives at the Vision Board Party. She is actually excited to make a vision board so she can visualize everything that she wants to happen in her life.

She walks into Nipsey's and looks around for signs of the event. All she sees is the bar area. Men and women sitting at the bar sipping, laughing and drinking. She asks herself, *Am I in the right place?*

A bartender standing behind the bar looks up from cleaning a glass and says, "Just head straight back. You will see it."

Karen smiles and thanks the gentleman. She walks towards the back where she can see a bright light ahead of her. When she steps outside, Karen looks around in awe. *Peaches really did her thing in here.*

The venue was gorgeous. There were round tables arranged all around the room. Each table was covered in a peach colored tablecloth trimmed in gold. Each table had a place setting for eight people. Each personalized gold placemat setting had a board set up on an easel for the participant to create their vision.

In the center of each table was a basket of supplies like scissors, glue sticks, rulers, washi tape and other craft supplies. There was a DJ on the stage playing soft jazz music to welcome the guests. On the left side of the venue, was a table of appetizers and small fruit trays.

On the opposite side of the venue, there were all the extra supplies needed for the board such as magazines, construction paper and decorative sheets of paper. The table on each centerpiece was a basket of peaches and flowers.

Peaches thought of everything. *She is so classy. She thinks of everything down to the last detail.* Karen thought.

There were several guests there when Karen arrived. They were walking around eating, drinking and socializing. Peaches was still running around getting things together. She threw her hand up at Karen to acknowledge her presence. Then she signaled for Karen to find her seat. So Karen walks around to find her name at a table.

While Karen is walking around the room, she is spotted by someone who recognizes her. Tessa recognizes Karen from the salon. While Tessa is a good friend of Sandy's, she is one of Lou's clients. Sandy is too busy with other things in her life to do Tessa's hair so she hooked Tessa up with Lou because she knows that Lou is the best.

Yes! Tessa smiles. She remembers Karen very well. She recalls all the times that Karen came sauntering through the shop with her nose in the air and monopolizing both Sandy and Lou's time. *That's the one who stressed Sandy out so much.*

Yes! I remember her. Tessa thinks. *I was in the shop under the dryer a few times when her fine ass husband came in to pay for her hair. Ooh and I* remember *that day he came in, barely spoke to her and went over to Lou's friend Charlice skinnin' and grinnin' all up in her face.* Tess saw that interaction between them. *Um humph!*

Being in the shop so often, Tessa has also heard many conversations between Sandy, Sam and Lou about Karen and her life with William and the kids. "I need to sit by this woman." Tessa mumbled to herself.

Tessa walks over to Karen. "Hey! I know you. You go to *Salon A'dore,* right?" She stands there smiling at Karen.

But Karen is standing there confused. She doesn't recognize Tessa. When Karen goes to the shop, she doesn't pay any attention to anyone. Karen only pays attention to herself because she knows the world revolves around her and only her. "Hi! Yes, I am a client of Lou's. I'm sorry. I do not recognize you. Do you work there?"

Tessa just looks at Karen. *As much as you are there, if I worked there you would recognize me.* "No! I am also a client of Lou's. I have seen you and your husband there several times. My name is Tessa. And you are...?" Tessa knows her name but she decides to play stupid like Karen.

"My name is Karen Lime. Um, do you know my husband?" Karen wants to know why this woman would bring up her husband.

Tessa quickly answers because she knows where Karen is going. She would hate for Karen to create an incident like

219

the one at the gala. "Oh no! No I don't. I just recall seeing him come into the shop to see you."

Because of Karen's reaction, Tessa decides not to tell Karen that she is a friend of Sandy's. Tessa has heard so many stories about Karen. She decided to take this time to get into Karen's head and find out Karen's side of the stories.

Tessa was so glad that Karen did not recognize her. I'm just going to sit back and take it all in. Peaches has actually placed Karen and Tessa at the same table.

Tessa is also friends with one of Peaches' clients. Tessa was at the gala. She saw everything that happened. Tessa called Sandy the next day and told her everything that happened. And of course Sandy told Sam. So the entire shop knew what happened at the gala. And Tessa could not wait to report the events of this party to Sandy.

Peaches walks over to Karen and Tessa. "Hey ladies! I am so glad that you two met. I want you all to meet Miss Hattie. I sat you three together because you all are going on the Girls' Cruise and I want all of my Girls to get to know each other. Let me walk you all to your table."

Peaches escorts the three ladies over to a table that has a cruise ship centerpiece. The ladies laugh because now Peaches' theme for this table makes sense. "Here you go ladies, Karen, don't forget to include pictures of family and children on your board. If that's what you really want."

Ms. Hattie is an older woman with plenty of money with no family. She was known for always hanging around the younger crowd. Ms. Hattie was known as a Negative Nancy. Nothing had gone right in her life except for the money she inherited years ago from her family.

All of the ladies at the table were going on the cruise. They discussed needing a break from family and work. They were all so excited.

Miss Hattie chimes in, "I don't know why y'all are so happy. You're just going to come home to the same old shit on a different day when you get back."

All of the women are silent except Karen. "Well when I come back, I am hoping that my husband will return home and we can go back to being a happy family again." She realizes what she said and goes on to explain. "Oh William and I are taking a break right now. Work was just so stressful to him. The kids and I were just too much so he went to stay with a friend for a while.

Tessa and the rest of the ladies looked at each other confused. But all said, "Oh okay!"

Ms. Hattie had something else to say, "Bullshit! Your husband is never coming home to you or your kids. He has had a taste of something good. Once a man gets something good, he never returns to the leftover garbage."

The other ladies at the table put their heads down or look away to avoid eye contact with both Karen and Miss Hattie.

Karen was in shock. She could not believe that Ms. Hattie was calling her garbage right to her face. Karen wanted to smack the taste out of the mouth of that old bitty but decided to remain cool because she is an old lady. Plus, she was at Peaches' event and she did not want to create a scene. *Old Bitty!*

Ms. Hattie is 83 years old. Although she looks like she is 70. She took really good care of herself. She works out five times a week. She doesn't date anyone over 70. She said that was her limit. All the men over 70 were way too old for her. And 70 was pushing it. "I am going to lower the age down to 65. No lower than 65 years old because I have to make sure they have money coming in like me."

Miss Hattie says her men have to have income to be around her. She doesn't want any broken energy. She was negative but not broke. She jumps Double Dutch every Sunday somewhere in Columbia, Maryland. Ms. Hattie never shared the details of her jumping. She didn't want too many people in her business. If they want to jump Double Dutch, they could find plenty of clubs online and social media platforms.

Miss Hattie tolerated this young group of women because she found them very entertaining and naive when it came to being real ladies. She knows they are all living in a pretend world that no one wants to leave. They love attention with social media, clothes, jewelry, hair, nails, you name it. She believed they had no real focus in life.

Every time someone at the table said something, Ms. Hattie would either have something negative to say or she would make the topic about her. Tessa and Karen both separately hope that Miss will not be around them on the cruise. She will spoil the entire girls trip with her funky attitude. *Where did Peaches find her?*

Tessa and Karen walk out of Nipsey's together. "That Miss Hattie is really going to test my faith on this cruise." Tessa declares.

Karen laughs, "You and me both. Did she have anything nice to say about anything this evening?"

"Umm!!" Tessa thinks. "I really don't think so. She was so busy complaining and bragging about all her men and their SSI checks."

"Girl you are hilarious. Maybe you and I can hang out on the cruise." Karen suggests.

"That would be cool." Tessa blurts out before she realizes what she has said. "I will see you soon Karen." Tessa hops in her car and drives away." She immediately calls Sandy.

Sandy answers, "Hey girl!" How was the party?"

"It was cool. Peaches sat me with your favorite former client and some old cougar lady named Hattie."

"Ooh! That sounds like an interesting combination. What was Karen lying about?" Asks Sandy.

"I can't really say that she was lying but she chose her words very carefully. I told her that I remember her from the shop but I didn't tell her how much I knew about her. But I got the impression that she thought I wanted her husband."

"Don't nobody want that man. I might let him get a taste though." Sam yells.

Tessa laughs, "Is that Sam yelling in the background?"

"Yes!" Sandy apologizes. "Sorry I have you on speaker. I am working on a client. I didn't think he was paying attention to me. So it was a nice party with no drama from Karen?"

"No! She was pretty cool. I think I might room with her on the cruise. We actually got along pretty well."

"NOOOOOO!!!!" Sam yells. "Don't do it! Do you recall the incident at the gala? You quickly forgot. That heifer might snap and throw you overboard. We done told you that she was crazy and shit. What if one of them people that she be talkin' to in her head tells her to push you overboard? Imma get up in front of your funeral and say I told her ass not to do it. I told her ass not to room with her. We told her." Sam starts fake crying and falling out like he is crying at a funeral.

The clients in the shop are cracking up at him acting silly.

"What is he doing?" Tessa asks.

"Acting a fool, as usual. Just be careful. That's all we are asking you to do. If there is someone else for you to hang out with, add that person to your duo."

"I hear you Sandy. I will give you a call later." They end the call.

Sam is jumping around, "I cannot wait for Kur'n to come in to get her hair done again. I am going in on her. I didn't mention the gala the last time she was here. But I'm finna go innnn. Y'all hear me team? I am going to put her ass on blast. When I finish with her, she ain't NEVER gonna wanna come in here again. Watch!"

The women in the shop discuss the gala and go around telling their stories about Karen. There are so many stories. Sam is taking it all in and adding it to his Kur'n collection for the next time.

"Writing fiction is the act of weaving a series of lies to arrive at a greater truth." — Khaled Hosse

Chapter XIII: *The Neglectful Whisper*

Careless Undertone

William saw all the signs that Karen was leaving around but he chose to ignore them because again he believed that Karen would not do anything to hurt her children. *She just wants attention and I will fall into her trap again.*

William saw the bottle of oxytocin pills that she left on the kitchen counter. He ignored that, even though he knew that the hospital did not prescribe them to her. *She wasn't in any physical pain. So why would she have these? Where would she get them from?* He did notice that it was a plain prescription bottle and the name had been crossed out with a dark black permanent marker.

Would she really go through with taking pills and killing herself over our relationship?

William takes the pills with him. *Maybe Karen will think that she misplaced the pills.*

William remembers that Karen is going on a fourteen day Girls Getaway with Peaches and some other women. "I think I will call Peaches and pick her brain. Maybe Peaches

226

knows more than I do. Perhaps she can help Karen."

Before he can call Peaches, his train of thought is interrupted by a call from Charlice. "Hey Babe! How is your day going?"

"I am having a wonderful day." Charlice replies ecstatic. "I just sold a five-million-dollar condo. My commission is going to be lovely. Lori has really been blessing me with these listings."

"That is wonderful, Babe. Congratulations" William is excited for her but is clearly irritated.

Charlice picks up on his somber tone, "Babe, are you okay? You sound sad."

"Mannn," he says before he realizes who he is talking to, "Sorry. Sorry. I didn't mean to address you in that manner. It's just that I am having a long day. Karen is not well. Mentally."

Ugggghhh! Here we go again. Charlice thinks. "What do you mean, Babe?" Charlice is tired of hearing about his family, their issues and his damn wife.

William is rambling on about Karen. He tells Charlice how worried he is about Karen because he found the pills on the kitchen counter and the name was blackened out. "I just don't know what to do because I know how manipulative she can be but this is a new trick for her. I want to know where she got those pills from. I don't want to ask her because if I do, she will know that I took them. And if this is a trick, she will think that I really care. I was thinking about calling Peaches just to pick her brain and see if she has any insight. I have to find a reason to call her. What do you think Babe? Do you think I should call Peaches or just leave it alone?"

Charlice ain't paying no attention to William. He basically ruined her exciting news with Poor Krazy Karen news. "Whatever you think is best? I have to go but I will see you tonight at the restaurant." She ends the call before he can say anything else.

"UGGGHHH!" Charlice screams out loud. *He is really struggling with his family affairs. I really don't want to deal with a man that has a crazy wife. I already dealt with a crazy man. Now this. I wonder how Guy is doing.*

Later that evening at dinner, William and Charlice get into a deep conversation about family.

William grabs Charlice's hands from across the table. "Charlice, I know I am asking a lot of you as I end my marital situation. And I ask again, please bear with me. I try to share everything with you because I want you to understand what I am dealing with and why it is not that simple for me to just walk away. I love you. I knew that I loved you from the moment that I saw you. Sometimes you just know. You are the first woman that has made me feel this way. I don't want to lose you." William stares deep into Charlice's eyes.

Charlice looks at William and sighs, "William, if I am being honest with you and myself, I am concerned. You and I have talked about my previous relationships. It seems like I never chose the available men. The question is are you truly available?"

William tries to interrupt her, "I a…"

"Stop! Let me finish." Charlice commands. "I never knew my father. So I know that it is very important that a father stay in their child's life. A child without a father never gets over that void. Maybe that is why I have always chosen unavailable men. Who knows? So I do understand why you are doing what you need to do. Let's see how things go and let's just enjoy ourselves."

William grabs Charlice's hands tighter. "Thank you Babe! I promise you, I have a plan and Karen will leave on her own. She will want to end this marriage by the time I am finished." William notices that Charlice did not give him a definitive answer but he will take it. I have asked a lot from her since we met. *I will prove myself to her.*

After dinner, William and Charlice decide that they will meet later at the house. Charlice's client is coming by the office to sign the papers for the $5 million deal. He had a late flight from Tokyo and did not want to wait until the morning to sign the papers.

William decides to go visit John to let him know that he took his advice. Plus, he needed a drink and some more advice from the man that knew him best. I *don't think John will mind if I drop by unannounced.* William is never surprised by what John may have going on. He can always expect the unexpected with John. But this time was different. Sam is there.

At John's house, William knocks once, then walks in, he stands in shock as he sees Sam laid back on the sofa, legs crossed holding a bourbon glass in his hand. William knows that Sam is gay but didn't realize that he may be in John's circle of friends. Then William starts to wonder: *Did Sam tell John about Karen? But then again I don't care; there isn't much to tell.* After his initial shock, William manages to belt out a, "Hey fellas! What's good?"

"Whoop! Speak of the devil." Sam whispers. "Hey William Lime How are you?"

"What's up, man?" John stands up to dap up his best friend.

William sits down in a chair and John passes him a drink that he just poured. "What a small world? How do you two know each other?"

"Seriously William?" Sam answers. "This is DC. Every gay, bisexual, transsexual, queer black male in DC knows each other. DC is literally a box."

The three men laugh at Sam's statement. Then Sam excuses himself. "I have a date. John I will fill you in with all the details later. William, it was nice talking to you. I will see you next week in the shop. Bye Gentlemen!"

"He is a character." John laughs. "What's up man? How is everything going? The last time I saw you, you were in limbo about your marriage and Charlice? Fill me in. What did you decide to do?"

Just before William arrived, Sam and John had an intense conversation about William and Charlice. Sam shared all of the shop gossip with John. John couldn't wait to hear William's interpretation of the situation.

***

After sitting with John for a while and sipping bourbon, Sam says, "You need to get your sexy BFF William Lime."

"Who, William?"

"Yes! He is a mess. He got these women dead confused about what he wants or rather who he wants. I don't even think he knows what he wants." Sam takes a sip of bourbon and leans back on the sofa.

John is confused. "What do you mean?"

"So let me break it down for you." Sam sits up. "Lou, the manager of the shop and a dear friend of mine, is best friends with Charlice, William's realtor." Sam put quotation marks up in the air around the term realtor. "Now Lou is also Karen's hairstylist. And when Karen comes in there, she always gives us a show and tries to make everybody feel like they are a piece of gum on the bottom of her shoe. We all call her Curiously Crazy Karen because

231

she is nosy, crazy and delusional."

John busts out laughing, "Is she that bad Sam?"

"YESS!!" Sam yells. "It is that bad. She really believes that she and William are going to get back together. She thinks that Charlice is just William's real estate agent. She thinks that William is still looking for a bigger house for her and the family. And William does not help the situation by coming in every other day to pay for her hair. Plus, he is sleeping with Charlice, as you may already know. If you ask me, he's crazy too."

"Oh so Karen doesn't even know that William purchased a new house in Largo for himself and the kids. And I think Charlice moved in with him."

"Yep! She sure did move in with him. I don't know why she did that because she is also dating a wealthy dude named Guy. At least, I think she is. I was with Charlice and Lou when she met him late one night in Chinatown. We went to get some Chinese food at around 1 am and he came strutting in with a group of men. The two of them locked eyes immediately. The first weekend that they met he took her on a weekend getaway to San Francisco. Lou and I thought she was going to move in with him because he gave her a Mercedes to drive. All I can say is that she must have something special between her legs if men are giving her $90,000 cars and leaving their entire families for her. Shoot I want some of that."

Sam falls over laughing. "I don't mean I want to get some. I mean I want some of what she has between her legs to get me some cars, trips, houses and lavish gifts."

John is falling out laughing. "I knew what you meant, Sam. You would never go that way."

"Well I did once. Tried it. Hated it. Never wanna see it, AGAIN. Too much work." Sam frowns up his face. "Let me tell you how it happened…"

That was all John heard about Sam's encounter with a woman. John starts to wonder if he knows Guy. *I know a man named Guy that deals in high end art. Could it be the same Guy? Guy is extremely private and travels the world a lot. He does live in the area somewhere. I'm not going to mention to Sam that I know of a man named Guy. I'm not going to speculate about Guy because I know what type of company Guy keeps. And I don't want him and his line of work to end up as part of the shop's gossip.*

The Guy that Sam knows has been dealing in high end art sculptures for years. He is known around the upscale areas. This Guy does not hang around in the downtown city areas of DC. So John is very surprised by how he ended up meeting Charlice unless she had some upscale clients. *Sam did say it was late at night. So maybe Guy was meeting a client or dealing art. Sam said he was with some other men.*

Just then Sam is interrupted by William walking in.

***

233

"Mannn," William starts. "I took your advice. Karen and I are in marriage therapy. We are also going as a family. Just in case things don't work out. I told Charlice about it and she is being supportive but she is also tired of hearing about Karen." William reaches into his pocket and pulls out the bottle of pills. "I found these on Karen's kitchen counter. I don't know what she is trying to do. I can't figure out if she is preparing to kill herself or if she is just trying to get attention. I don't know what to think."

After listening to William and considering what Sam had told him, John realizes that William is way in over his head. "You just need to slow down. Take your time with the therapy. Take your time with Charlice. You have time to figure this out." John thought about telling William that Charlice is seeing someone else and he needs to be careful but he decides that he best stay out of this. There is too much at stake for everyone involved if he starts snitching and asking questions. *I wonder if William knows about the other man.*

"You are right, John. I will slow it down. I don't want to lose Charlice though. But I will make it work. Thanks friend. I appreciate you."

William stands up and gives John a hug. The two men talk a little more about politics and life. Then William leaves.

After William and Sam leave, John starts thinking about what Sam shared about Charlice and Guy. *This could not be Guy Vanders; it just couldn't be. If Charlice is involved with Guy, she is way over her head. She just came to town, and has no idea who she may be involved with.*

People today are too quick to dive into relationships with people without truly getting to know the person. "This is bad."

John thinks, *Let me call Kitty and see if she has heard from or seen Guy. She would know if anyone.*

John calls Kitty in San Francisco. "Hey Kitty! How have you been?"

"John? I am well. No complaints. How are you? It has been a minute since we have spoken. What is going on in the DMV?"

"Nothing much. Nothing much. I was just thinking about taking a trip to San Francisco and I wanted to see if you were still running your bed and breakfast. I wanted to be somewhere peaceful so that I could get some work done."

Kitty was excited. "Oh my goodness! You too! Guy was just out here with a beautiful young lady." Kitty was surprised. "If you bring someone out here, please make sure she knows your last name. That chick Guy brought didn't even know his last name. I thought that was a little strange. I had never known Guy to bring any lady to the bed and breakfast. It appeared as if they didn't know each other that well."

"I wouldn't do that Miss Kitty. In this game, you have to be

235

careful. You can't bring anyone near the circle."

"I know that's right." Kitty thinks, "Has Guy gone mad? He has never done this before. Should I try to talk to Guy?" *Guy is different. I don't know how he will respond.*

Thank Miss Kitty. I need to make arrangements with my travel agent. She or I will make the necessary arrangements. Good Bye!" *I'm not going there. Guy has compromised the location.*

John's suspicions are now confirmed. He can't tell anyone, definitely not Sam. Sam loves to talk. He can't even warn William at this point. John decided to let this scenario play out. He is going to stay low. *I need to leave the country for a while.*

***

The second counseling session did not go well at all. The counseling session goes left because Dr. Wells brings up baggage that Karen did not want to talk about. Dr. Wells talks to each family member individually. She speaks to Willow first. Then Will Jr. followed by Karen and then William Sr, last. Dr. Wells wants to get each one's story before she brings them together as a family unit.

Willow and Dr. Wells talk about Karen and Karen's childhood. Willow is concerned about how her mother's childhood affects her mother now. Like the marriage and how she raises them. She also expresses how she feels left out by her dad. She feels like dad loves Will J. more than her.

Dr. Wells writes this all down and notes: **Willow is angry. She feels neglected. She is concerned for her mom's mental health.**

Will J. is just loving life. He wants to live in the house as a family like they used to do. He wishes Willow liked him and he wants her to stop saying that dad is not his dad.

Dr. Wells notes: **Will J. wants his family to be whole. Does not like them apart. Wants to improve his relationship with Willow. Is he William's son?**

Dr. Wells calls William back next. "So William, let's talk about your childhood."

"With all due respect Dr. Wells, I am not here to talk about that. Let me tell you what I want to talk about. I do not want to be here. I am here because I need for you to conclude that my wife and I should get a divorce. My wife needs therapy. She is mentally unstable. She needs more than a marriage counselor." *I'm not going to tell Dr. Wells about the pills. She will have us in her forever.*

"I understand that you don't want to be here Mr. Lime but at the end of the day we are here for your children. You agreed to do the family counseling for them; not for yourself. The quicker you come with a better attitude, the quicker you get out of counseling. Now I am going to ask you again, how was your childhood?"

William rolls his eyes but answers, "It was interesting. Because of that experience, I am protective of my children. I have to make sure that they are happy. I thought that Karen was going to be the perfect wife and mother because of her own childhood trauma but she was affected far more than I had initially realized."

"Oh? What do you mean William?" Dr. Well asks.

"All throughout our marriage she has done things to manipulate situations and to manipulate me. She is always the victim. People are always doing something to her. I am tired of looking the other way and cleaning up her mess. But I walk cautiously because I am unsure of how much she can handle mentally."

"I understand William. The idea is to get everyone to a state of acceptance. We have to get everyone on the same page. Okay?"

Dr. Wells' notes: **William hidden trauma that he is not ready to reveal. Wants to leave the marriage but does not want to hurt his children. More family therapy is needed.**

"So Karen, let's talk about your parents. From what you can remember, how was your mom and dad's relationship?" Dr. Wells sits back and looks at Karen.

Karen just sits there staring at Dr. Wells. This is not why she is here. Karen wants the counseling sessions but she doesn't know if she is ready to open up about everything. There is some hesitation about moving forward. Karen knows that she must open up if she wants to have William back. "My mother killed my dad. I don't remember what their relationship was like. I thought they were happy. I thought we were a happy family."

Dr. Wells is speechless. She writes: **Karen...TRAUMA. Psychiatrist needed immediately. Additional support needed. Marriage counseling? Not ready for a divorce.**

"Okay Karen! I will not ask you any more questions about your childhood. Just tell me what you want to gain from therapy."

Karen starts sobbing. "I want my husband back home. I want my happy family back. I want you to tell William that he needs to come home to work on our marriage. How can we work on our marriage in separate homes?"

"Karen, I know that is what you want but we have to get to that point. A lot has happened in your marriage that needs to be addressed. You and your husband can try dating again. You have to relearn each other. Now I need you to put all of that aside. I am going to bring the family in so that we can talk together." Dr. Wells steps out to get the family.

This session is way too long. Karen thinks. *I need to go get myself together. I need to pack for the cruise, get my hair*

done before I leave. I hope Lou has some openings. This
may take some time.

The voice in her head starts to talk to her: *You are wrong*
on so many levels for the manipulation of a good
relationship. You can be so selfish and insensitive. When
are you going to do right by others? You have a family to
think about but you only think about yourself.

"I do not." Karen answers the voice. "Everything that I do I
do for my children and my husband."

Karen loves her children and always took them on vacation.
Karen loves to cruise because there was so much for her
family to do on the ship. This trip was the first one that she
has been on without her children and/or her husband. She
did need to do something for herself. "Don't try to make
me feel guilty about trying to do something for myself."
Karen yells at the voice in her head.

Just then the family walks into the room.

Willow speaks first, "Mom, who the heck are you yelling at
now?"

Karen laughs, "I was just yelling out loud. It seems like we
have been here all day."

Dr. Well interrupts, "Come one everybody. Let's all sit
down and talk a little bit."

Willow and Will J. each take a chair which leaves Karen
and William to sit on the sofa together. William sits down

and Karen sits down right up under him. William tries to move over but she does not leave him any room.

"After meeting with you all individually, I think that we have a lot of work to do. You all have genuine concerns about your roles in the family and your perception of things. I think that we should begin meeting 3 days a week. One day with the children. One day with the parents and the third day will be all of us together."

"WHAT?" The Limes yell out together surprised.

"Yes! If I could manage it, I would meet with you all every day. Listen, each of you just think about the conversations that we had alone. Think about your concerns. In order to resolve your individual problems, we need to meet every week. One session a week is not going to be enough. Understand?"

They all shake their heads yes.

"Good! Good!" Dr. Wells is pleased. "So today we can talk about the children. So Will J. how was school this week?"

Will J. starts to talk about his week. He is so happy to have someone listen to him.

Willow is mad that she has to listen to him speaking. *How is this important to my life and fixing our family? Are we going to talk about who his real father is?*

William is thinking the same thing. *I love my son but right now I don't care about his day. I am reading to see my*

241

baby. I hope she is waiting for me in bed. I hope I can survive this therapy. If I don't see any progress in a month, we are out. I am going to be out.

Karen hopes that once she returns from her cruise the next session will be more productive. She is just sitting there with a smile on her face looking at William in a loving way. *Oh I hope this works out for us. After the cruise, I will be all in and reading to work on my marriage.*

The Limes talk to Dr. Wells a little bit more. They set up their next appointments and leave.

Dr. Wells writes her notes. **The Limes: EVERYONE needs therapy. The parents have each experienced some type of trauma that needs to be addressed. Recommend therapy for each of them. Family therapy is definitely recommended. This is going to take time. Lord help us all.**

"One whisper, added to a thousand others, becomes a roar of discontent"— Julie Garwood

Chapter XIV: The Solitude Getaway

Isolated Escape

Karen needs this Girls Trip because of everything that was going on.

She is all packed. She called Lou yesterday after the therapy session. Lou has a 10:00am appointment available. Karen must get her hair done before she goes on vacation. "I cannot go anywhere with my hair looking like this."

Karen arrives at the shop at 9:55am. Lou has one client before her so she has to wait. Karen hates to wait. She prefers to come straight in the salon and sit right in the chair. Well not today. So she sits down in Lou's other chair hoping to speed Lou up.

Sam is in the back with Sandy when he hears Karen. Sam looks at Sandy, grabs her hand and says, "Let's go get her. I have been waiting for her all morning." Today, Sam is ready for Karen. He has been waiting to have this conversation. He wonders if Karen will bring up the gala. If she doesn't, he sure will.

Sandy really does not want to see or hear Karen. Sandy has been over Karen for months. To Sandy, Karen was extremely draining both emotionally and financially. Karen has cost Sandy so much. She had lost clients because of her. Sandy wanted to stay far-far away from Karen.

Karen's energy was not good for her mentally. Sandy knew that Sam had been dying for the perfect opportunity to get back at Karen so she decided to be Sam's support. No one could forget that day Karen went off on Sam. *Sam was as quiet as a church mouse after she finished berating him. Poor Sam; he was so embarrassed that day. I could see the tears in his eyes.* Sandy doesn't know how this encounter is going to turn out, but she knows deep down inside, it's not going to go well.

Sam never forgot that dreadful day back in November when Karen was on her high horse. She tore into Sam like a machete cuts flesh. She pranced into the shop and told him about just how jealous he was of her and how he wished he could be a real woman like her.

Karen told Sam that he was lonely and pathetic. She said, "Men like you will always be lonely because you are miserable being a man and miserable because you can never be a woman. You will just be living a miserable little life trying to fit in somewhere. You will never have family and the family you have doesn't want you and never did."

When Sam talked to John the other night, he got the real tea about her and William and how William feels about her. William does not want Karen at all. He is going through the motions to keep her sane.

"Ooh hey Kar'n! I thought I heard you. How are you today?" Sam says.

"Oh hi Sam! I am wonderful today. I am getting ready to leave for my Girls Cruise."

Karen can sense that Sam's attention towards her is disingenuous. *Not today. I have had enough of him.* She thinks. Karen has a lot on her mind and she is starting to feel overwhelmed with everything that is happening in her life.

The therapy sessions are not going the way she wants them to go. She thought Peaches would have put in a good word. She had expected Dr. Wells to do the bare minimum, not her full-fledged job. *This bitch is trying to dig too deep into my life and my past. Why would she do that? Why would Peaches do this to me knowing what I want and what I have going on right now. Peaches claims to be my friend but after this little stunt she has pulled, I am starting to think otherwise. Is Peaches trying to sabotage my marriage? I am definitely going to have a heart to heart, one on one conversation with Ms. Peaches on this cruise. I don't need this! That's not what I want right now. I just need my husband back home with the family. Then this "Sam I Am" wants to fuck with me early this morning. I don't feel like talking or discussing anything. I just need my hair done. But here he comes stirring the pot.*

"Oh that sounds fabulous. But you didn't finish telling us all the juicy details about the Gala. You didn't have a lot of time when you were here a few days ago. I heard it was full of fireworks. I heard that there was a shooting and I heard that you were all balled up in a corner in a fetal position crying like a baby screaming' DADDY! DADDY!' You didn't tell us none of that. Then I heard that they had to take you out in an ambulance to the psych ward? Kar'n, how could you forget to tell us all about that? You're so pathetic KaREN. So called women like you who try to be something they are not end up living lonely lives without their husbands or families. They just get tired of living MISERABLE lives with PATHETIC ass people. Wouldn't you agree KaREN?" Sam places his hands on his hip and looks side eyed at Karen.

Karen was speechless. She didn't know what to say. Where did he get all this accurate information? Who was his source? Sam and Lou never travel in the same circles as her.

Why is he doing this? I am going to keep this fake ass smile on my face until I get out of here. He is really pushing my buttons.

Karen awkwardly laughs, "Who told you all of this, Sam? You cannot believe everything you hear. After all, you were not there. Were you?"

Sam says, "No Karen! So YOU tell me what happened?"

He can't be serious right now. Karen is about to blow. She continues to smile as if Sam is a little puppy, and she wants to pat him on his head and tell him to fetch a bone or a man. Karen stands up to pat him.

By this time, Lou is ready for Karen to sit in her chair. "Come on Karen. Sit her. Just ignore Sam." Lou already knows everything because Charlice tells her everything that William tells her.

"Sam, can you go check the towels in the dryer, please?" Lou asked. If they are dry, please and put them away. After that, can you refill all the shampoo and conditioner bottles for me? We are running low at the shampoo stations."

Lou makes Sam leave Karen alone while she tries to do her hair. He is agitating Karen and Lou won't have him messing with her money.

When Lou has almost finished Karen's hair, Sam sees his opportunity to start again. "So Kar'n, let's hear your side of the story. What happened? Were you balled up in the corner or not? Was you crying and screaming? Did you go to the Loony Bin or not? Spill the tea, woman."

Karen is still trying to maintain her composure. She thought Sam would have let this go by now. She thinks, *Let me answer the many questions he has and hopefully he will leave me alone.*

"Sam, yes there was a shooting. All the rest of your story is an exaggeration. It was a figment of someone's imagination. I went to the spa after the shooting. I needed a mental health retreat." Karen is speaking calmly to Sam but she is visibly getting upset.

Lou can see it in her face and asks the receptionist to bring Karen a glass of wine.

Sam falls out laughing, "BITCH, you were NOT at the spa. You were in the MFin' loony bin because something happened to your daddy when you were little. Something about you and those gunshots or perhaps you just balled up because your husband don't want you. He's tired of you and just wants you to ball up and go away. Stop playing with us Kar'n. You know damn well that everybody in the DMV is talkin' bout you at the gala. And talkin' bout your sexy ass husband leaving you. Tell the truth for once. Get out of your fantasy world."

Sam feels so good and vindicated at this moment. He was on get-back-mode and he conquered the task of tearing into her just like she did him a few months back. Karma will come for you when you least expect it. He was smiling like a lion that had just cornered his prey in a corner with no space to run or hide. *I got this bitch now. Yeah, you wanted to come for me and thought I was going to let you get away with belittling me in front of the whole shop. My work place… where I have to come every day to earn a living. K'urn you got the game fucked up. Let's see how you come back from this.* Sam smiled to himself.

Karen jumps up out of Lou's chair. Rips the black nylon cape off her chest. She is pissed. She even made Sam jump back.

"Listen here Sam. I am tired of you always coming for me. I have had enough." Karen is screaming at the top of her lungs. "I already told you that I was at the spa. When the shooting happened, I ducked down like everyone else does when someone starts shooting. I'm tired of being the butt of your jokes. You aren't even on my level. You are BENEATH me."

Karen takes a deep breath and the salon is silent. "If it wasn't for your father, she never would have killed my father. He would still be here to protect me from people like this. If it wasn't for you, she would be here to protect me. I HATE YOU SERGIO!" Karen grabs her handbag and runs out of the salon.

The salon is at a standstill. No one is moving. No one is saying a word. *What just happened?* Everyone is thinking.

Sam stomps his foot, looks out the window towards Karen and yells. "WHO THE HELL IS SERGIO?"

Everyone in the shop burst out laughing and the chatter began. Lou just shakes her head.

"You didn't have to do her like that, Sam." Lou looks away from him.

Lou is really feeling sorrying for Karen. She knows Karen can be difficult at times, but she realizes that Karen is going through a lot right now. Lou starts to think of her own life right now. *Damn, I am dealing with my own issues and this new relationship. Everything is weighing down on me right now. I can't imagine how Karen is feeling right now. And I hate being in the middle of all of this mess. I am trying to get my life together and everybody wants to bring me their problems. I should have stayed in school and become a psychologist or psychiatrist.*

Charlice has told me everything and I still can't come to terms with sharing my current situation. I will tell her soon before big mouth Sam spills the hot tea. Amber keeps asking me about Charlice and I told her she will meet my sister-friend in the near future. Amber seems to think that Charlice and I were physically intimate which is just a crazy thought. I wonder where Amber really lives. Since we have been dating, I have never been to her place in Chicago. She continues to make excuses or she always ends up here at my place. I guess she has to meet Charlice and feel her out for herself. Then hopefully we can move past the insecurities.

Lou knew Charlice would be fine with Amber. Charlice isn't around that much anyway since she has been seeing William and working.

Lou has always been the rock of her family and has always supported her mother, even though her mother never really supported her. Well, giving her mother grace, her mother did not know how to support her. After the family visit, she knew and understood that her mother was on survival mode.

"Lou stop." Sam says. "Everyone, including you, is tired of her coming in here acting like she is better than all of us. We all have been victims of trauma and we all have our own triggers. Us women of color are supposed to uplift each other. I decided to hold her accountable today."

"But Sam, clearly she is not ready to face her trauma."

"Well dammit, I helped her today. You see, I helped her release Sergio. Look at me. Now I'm a therapist and a spiritual healer. I released the demon, Sergio from her body. Umm Shock lock Umm!" Sam starts walking around the room shaking his body like a flying bird.

Lou and the rest of the shop patrons are laughing at him. "Stop Sam. Just stop. You have met your ignorance quota for the day." Lou yells at him.

Karen now knows that she really needs a getaway. She is still in disbelief. She was so embarrassed at the salon. *How could Sam make up those lies and tell everyone about me being in the psych ward?* She didn't know how she was going to handle the gossip when she returned.

This cruise Peaches has planned is perfect. Peaches has planned a girl's trip on a fourteen-day cruise. Karen wants to get her thoughts together. She wants to come back refreshed and ready to work on her family. When she returns, William should have the house ready for her and the children. While she is away she will think about seeking help for her past traumas especially after the incident in the salon. *Did I really call Sam, Sergio?*

***

William purchased tickets for him and Charlice to see the violinist, Damien Escobar at Wolf Trap. Since it is his weekend with the children, he hires a babysitter company to watch Willow and William Jr.

Willow is pissed. "I am too old for a babysitter. I prefer to go over to one of my friends' houses. Are you serious, dad?"

"Yes, I am serious." William replies. "I am not okay with that because I don't know any of the parents of your friends nor do I know their families for that matter."

Willow stomps up the stairs to her room and slams the door, while William greets the babysitter.

William and Charlice attend the concert at the Wolf Trap. They have a wonderful time. It was so romantic. The evening reminds Charlice of the reasons why she wants to be with William.

After the concert, they stop at a small local restaurant near the concert venue.

"I had a wonderful time tonight, William. Thank you." Charlice leans over and kisses William passionately on the lips.

"I am so glad you had a great time Babe. You deserve it. I

haven't been the best man for you but I promise you that you won't regret choosing to be with me."

"By the way," William recalls. "I know I mentioned it but Karen goes on her cruise next week. I decided to stay at the home in DC so I don't interrupt their routines during the two weeks that their mother will be gone. So are you going to stay at the house alone?"

Charlice just looks at him. Dumbfounded. Charlice feels some kind of way because she has not met the kids yet. "Every time I am supposed to meet your children something happens. I am beginning to think that you really don't want me to meet your children and/or you are having second thoughts."

"Babe, it's not that I don't want you to meet them. It's just that I don't think the time is right. We are in therapy. I just feel like we need to wait."

William thinks to himself, *why can't Charlice understand what I am going through as a family man? I need her to be here for me because this is a lot to handle. And having her in my life has really eased some pressure, physically and emotionally. If Karen was half the woman Charlice was, I would still be at home. What good family man wants to get up and leave their home? If Charlice has a little patience, all this will be over soon, I know she loves me but…*

"William, you are about to have the kids for over two weeks and I'm still not able to meet them? Make it make sense please? Here I am living in your house and sleeping in your bed and I haven't met your kids yet." Charlice wants to understand but it's hard for her to understand because of her past relationship with Doug.

"Okay Charlice! Point taken. You are correct. I will tell Willow and Will J. about you. Then I will let you meet them." *It's time and I don't want it to be a surprise to them when they come over to the house and find her there. Then again, maybe I should wait until the counseling sessions are over? I will think about it again before the kids return home back to their mother at the end of her trip. Suppose I decide I want to give my family and wife another chance? Hum?*

William and Charlice end up back at their home in Largo. Charlice stays the night with the kids there. Usually she would go stay at a hotel or go stay at Lou's but William said it would be okay as long as she stays in the room until the children leave.

In the morning, William takes the children to school and Charlice stays in bed until she hears them driving away. *Let's see if he keeps his word this time.*

After William drops the children off, he goes to the house to get Karen. William takes Karen to the Baltimore port. Karen cries all the way to the port.

William rolls his eyes, "Why are you crying Karen? You will only be gone for two weeks. The children are going to be at your house with me. I am going to sleep in the guest room. We will continue to attend counseling. You are going on the Girls Cruise with your friends to get away. To Relax-Refresh-Release-Reset. Enjoy yourself!"

"I know but…" Karen can't speak from crying. Karen knew William would pick up with the family counseling session since the marriage counseling session could not happen without her.

William assures her the kids are going to be fine with him for two weeks. "The kids will be fine. Stop worrying so much about them."

Part of the reason Karen was crying was because she was thinking about what happened at the shop. *How could I let Sam take me there? I don't remember what I even said to him. Oh my God, I have to apologize to Lou when I get back. She may never want to do my hair again. I am going to have to find a new salon soon. I will ask Peaches where she gets her hair done. I may need a new scene now. There are way too many Envious Eves at the salon. I need this cruise before I lose it.*

"William, are you going to miss me while I am gone?"

William hears Karen but he refuses to answer her because his answer is no. He just wants her to go on this trip and clear her mind. He just remembers that he forgot to call Peaches about the pills that he found. He decides to give her a call after he drops Karen off. "I thought Peaches was supposed to bring you to the port. What happened?"

"She had too much to do before we boarded so it just did not work out."

Yes, Karen was going to ride in with Peaches and yes Peaches had a lot to do so she didn't want to commit to picking up Karen. But, Peaches also did not want to hear about William all the way to the Baltimore port, which was almost an hour from Karen's house. She just couldn't take it today. She had too much on her mind.

When they arrive at the port, there is a group of women that are getting ready to board the cruise ship in Baltimore.

William pulls up to where he sees a lot of people. He takes Karen's suitcases out of his truck. He says, "Okay Karen! There you are." He leans over for a side hug but she meets him with a kiss on the lips. "I will see you here in two weeks. Have fun. Get some rest."

Why would she do this? Am I sending her all the wrong signals? William is thinking why would Karen think it was okay to kiss him in the mouth. They have not kissed or been intimate in months.

"William, I love you. When I come back, I will be a new me. I will return as the wife that you want me to be. I promise." Karen heads towards the ship pulling her bags behind her.

William gets back in his truck as he watches her board the

ship. Then he calls Peaches. "Hey Peaches! Are you ready for this trip?"

"Hey William! Yes, I am so ready for this trip. Two weeks on multiple islands with my girls and sexy men at every port…I'm more than ready."

William laughs, "I am not mad at you. I just dropped Karen off. I am a little worried about her. She was crying. Can you check in on her for me please? I don't think she has been away from the kids for this length of time."

"Of course, I will look after her. That is my girl. I will check in on her as soon as I get settled."

"Wonderful! I appreciate you for being there for her. She is blessed to have a friend like you to support her through everything. You both deserve to have a great time. I will see you when you get back."

If Peaches really was Karen's friend, William hoped that Peaches would be there for her and truly understand Karen. Karen had a lot of layers and looking back, he wasn't sure how he managed to be with her this long. He knew it was about his kids. He wasn't sure if Karen shared her whole life story with Peaches. Karen couldn't have shared everything with Peaches. If so, Peaches would have eased away from the friendship long ago.

"Okay William. Take care of yourself and those kids." Peaches says and ends the call. She thought perhaps William was calling her because he knew about the envelope that her PI friend gave her. She didn't have time to open it now. She was just pulling up to the port. *I will open it later. Everything done in the dark always comes to the light Mr. Lime. I hope he doesn't think it's okay to call or text me on this trip to check on his wife. We are not doing that!!! I have done my job by referring them to the best therapist in town. As a matter of fact, let me block his number temporarily just in case. Wait! Let me block all the unwanted callers. Everybody wants a taste of Peaches.* She laughs to herself.

After William drops Karen off and heads back to DC, he stops by a Walgreens to pick up a DNA home test. William is going to put an end to all his doubts and fears about William Jr. *I have to know once and for all. Will this really make me feel better knowing if he is really my son? How would I feel knowing that he may not be my son? Can I honestly say that I would treat him the same knowing that he is not my son? How will I explain this to Willow? Maybe, I should let Karen explain it to her. Karen put us all in this situation.* William's head is spinning with all the unanswered questions. William did not realize how much of a toll this was taking on his work life. He hasn't had the time to focus on his professional commitments. He didn't notice that he had missed so many emails that were attached to deadlines.

"No matter how far you travel, you can never get away from yourself. It's like your shadow. It follows you everywhere. -Komura"— Haruki Murakami, After the Quake

Chapter XV: Hysterically Stranded

Uncontrolled Trap

"Damn!" Peaches shouts after she opens up the envelope that she received from one of her private investigator friends in DC. She is looking at pictures of William and Charlice at Wolf Trap laid out on the lawn snuggled up together on a blanket with a basket of wine and cheese sitting in front of them. William was holding Charlice so close. Peaches knew this was more than a business relationship.

Peaches had promised Karen that she would do some digging into this Charlice girl and she did just that. Now Peaches was not sure if she would tell Karen because she told Karen that William wasn't cheating. She had constantly reassured Karen that William was not cheating. She truly believed that he was being faithful and to now find out that he was really cheating all along. *I feel so bad for Karen.*

"I don't know what to do." Peaches debates. "Should I tell her now or should I wait until we return home so that Karen can enjoy herself on this cruise."

Just then Khrystina walks up, "Peaches, who are you talking to? She asks.

Peaches laughs, "Myself girl." She shows Khrystina the pictures of William and Charlice. "Should I tell Karen now or should I wait until after the cruise?"

"Good question. I think you should wait until after the cruise. We are having so much fun now. Why ruin it with sad news? She is going to be really sad when she sees these pictures."

"You're right. I will wait. Let's leave all the drama on the mainland."

***

Tessa and Karen are on the same floor, but their rooms are not close at all. Tessa's room is in the back of the ship. And Karen's room is in the front of the ship.

Tessa and Karen decide that they will develop a routine to meet up for breakfast every morning at 7 am. Since the buffet area is not crowded around this time, they will get a chance to talk in private about their lives.

Tessa and Karen make plans to spend a lot of time together on and off the ship. They decide to do some of the same excursions.

Tuesday: Day 1- At Sea- 4pm Departure

Tessa and Karen spend some of the evening separately resting and unpacking in their cabins.
They arrive at the safety test deck at the same time. Since everyone has to take the test before the ship leaves the port, they decide to get it over with as soon as possible. After

the safety test, Karen and Tessa stay out on the deck and have a seat by the pool.

As the two ladies sit and get more acquainted, Karen starts talking about her family. "I don't know how I am going to make it all this time without my husband and children. I have never slept alone this many nights without my William by my side." She sighs. Then continues, "I mean William and I have been having problems the past few months but we are working things out. We started marriage counseling and family counseling to try to fix what is broken. I hope this trip helps both William and I understand how important we are to each other. You know absence makes the heart grow fonder. So they say." She crosses her fingers. "How about you Tessa? What do you have going on back home? A man? A woman? Children?"

Tessa laughs, "Karen you are crazy. I have a little male friend that I have been seeing for a while. Our relationship is perfect the way it is. We are just enjoying each other's company. I have two God children. I have never had that motherly instinct to want children. I am content with spoiling my God children then returning them back to their parents."

"Oh my goodness!" Karen exclaims, "My life would not be complete without my children and my husband. They make me who I am. My husband is my soulmate. He is the love of my life. I understand him needing a break from the family dynamics. I respect that and I honor his request because I love him so much."

Khrystina finally comes down to take her safety test. She sits down and joins Karen and Tessa's conversation.

Khrystina sits and just listens in for a while then she walks off. She decides that she would like to engage in a more diverse conversation instead of the one Tessa and Karen are engaged in. After all she is on vacation for relaxation not to listen to someone's woes. *Peaches is such a saint for being a dear friend to Karen. Karen is definitely a handful.*

"Hey Khrystina! Where is Peaches?" Tessa asks. Tessa would like to change the conversation topic as well.

Khrystina turns back. "She is handling some last minute business. She won't be doing a safety test. Peaches feels like she has been on too many cruises to keep taking the safety tests. They know her by now." *Poor Karen.* Khrystina thinks as she recalls the pictures that Peaches shared with her before they boarded the ship. *Here she is talking about her husband like he walks on water and he is back home carrying on an affair. So sad. I feel so sorry for her.*

Wednesday: Day 2- At Sea

Tessa and Karen plan to spend the day at the spa.

They meet for breakfast in the main dining room. They are really bonding. Tessa feels like all the ladies, including Sam and Sandy, have Karen all wrong. *Karen is a really nice and cool person to hang out with. She isn't crazy or at least she hasn't shown me any signs of craziness or selfishness.*

After a relaxing day at the spa, the duo decides to spend a little time in the casino.

As they are strolling through, they see Miss Hattie at a slot machine.

"Oh there goes Miss Hattie. Hey Mi…" Tessa starts but is interrupted by Karen pulling her in the other direction.

"Uh uh! Uh uh!" Karen shakes her head and pulls Tessa away and not making eye contact with Miss Hattie. *I cannot take Miss Hattie right now.* Karen thinks.

Ms. Hattie sees them before they can get out of sight. "Girls come on over here." Ms. Hattie is sitting really close to an older gentleman. He is just Miss Hattie's type of man older than Karen and Tessa but younger than Miss Hattie.

Tessa and Karen look at each other thinking, *Damn! She saw us.* The duo turn around and in unison they say, "Hey Miss Hattie!"

"Come on over here and meet my new friend, Desmond. I met him at the gym." Grasping the man's shoulder, Hattie says, "Desmond, meet the girls." Miss Hattie spends a lot of her time at the gym and the casino. That is where she meets her male friends or at least that is what she told them at dinner last night.

Desmond looks a little too comfortable with Miss Hattie but he looks the women up and down, "Hey pretty ladies! How are y'all doing?"

Tessa answers first, "We are well. We must go now. We are headed to the stage show. Miss Hattie, we will see you later. Desmond, it was a pleasure meeting you." Tessa grabs Karen's arm to whisk her away. Karen just smiles and nods.

Karen laughs, "Thank you, Tessa! You are a lifesaver."

"I try." Tessa laughs. Then the two laugh together, play a few slots and go off to the stage show.

Thursday: Day 3-At Sea

Tessa and Karen spend the day at the casino. They both earn enough points for a free cruise. They go to the future cruise desk to find out about booking another cruise.

"Ooh!" Karen says, "I think I am going to book a cruise for my family." She considers getting a suite because she knows that William will be fully vested in their marriage and family. "I am only going to book a seven-day cruise because William has to work. He cannot spend too much time away from his job. He is too important."

Tessa, concerned, asks, "Do you think it is a good idea? You know booking the family cruise not knowing what may happen?"

Karen looks at Tessa perplexed by Tessa's question. "Yes! It will be okay. Hubby and the kids will enjoy the family getaway." *What is wrong with her? Is she just jealous of me because I have a family and she doesn't?*

Friday: Day 4-Charleston, SC

The ship pulls up and docks in Charleston, South Carolina.

Tessa and Karen visit the famous seafood restaurant and the market that sells all the gifts and jewelry.

Tessa picks up some items to buy as gifts and souvenirs for her God children. Karen purchases a beautiful silver butterfly necklace and ring set for Willow.

The ladies discuss the fact that they have not seen much of Peaches during this trip except for the occasional times at lunch or dinner. The two of them are really getting along. Karen is so happy that she has someone else to bond with given the fact that Peaches is so busy.

Tessa is also glad that she has found a friend on this cruise.

Saturday: Day 5- Miami, FL

Today the ladies plan to get off the ship to attend a yacht party hosted by Peaches. The mayor arranged the party for Peaches and ladies to attend.

Before they go to the party, Tessa wants to shop at a few TJ Maxx and Ross stores. "I heard that Miami has the best TJ Maxx and Ross stores in the country. And there are so many of them."
"Really?" Karen asks. "I didn't know that."

"Yes, girl." They carry the same designers like Gucci, YSL, Prada, Fendi, and all others like the high end stores." Tessa answers. "Why would I spend my money on the high end stores when I can get the same items cheaper?"

"I guess." Karen answers skeptically. "The items are old and out of season. Who wants to carry designers out of season?" Karen laughs. "You just look broke and thirsty." Karen frowns her face. *I can't believe that Tessa likes to shop at those hand me down stores.* "I wouldn't be caught dead in those stores."

Tessa just stands there looking at Karen, disgusted by her comments. *Let me get away from this woman before I say something that I can't take back. I can no longer accompany Karen on this cruise. She is way too judgmental.* "I will see you later Karen. I am going shopping." Tessa walks away from Karen as Karen is still talking to her.

Tessa sees Khrystina as she is heading off the ship. "That damn Karen has lost her mind and I can no longer be in her presence."

"Oh my!" Khrystina responds. "I am so sorry to hear that. We still have a few days on the ship. Perhaps you two can meet at a common ground before we get off the ship in Baltimore."

"Humph! I doubt it." Tessa leaves the ship.

While in Miami, she calls Sandy. "Hey Sandy! I just called to tell you that you were right. Karen is crazy. I gave her the benefit of the doubt and I tried to get to know her but the whole time she kept saying slick shit out her mouth. I couldn't take it anymore. She was about to make me lose my religion."

"I told you." Sandy laughs. "I told you that her elevator doesn't go all the way to the top. She had me thinking that I was crazy. But she is the problem. Girl, enjoy your trip. Call me when you get back. Love you!"

Tessa goes to TJ Maxx and Ross, alone. She finds so many designer clothing and accessories. *Everybody was right. Miami has the best stores.* By the time she is finished shopping, it is time for her to return back to ship to prepare for the yacht party.

When Tessa is back on the ship, she cancels all of her excursions with Karen. "Not today, Ma'am. I served my time with that woman."

At the yacht party, Peaches looked gorgeous in her light peach ensemble. Karen spent most of the party up under Peaches and running errands for her. She attempts to talk to Tessa a few times but Tessa keeps blowing her off. She tells herself, *Tessa must be going through some things right now. I will give her some space and time.*

Tessa does everything she can do to avoid Karen. She even sat and talked to Miss Hattie to avoid Karen. Tessa prides herself on living a drama free non-judgmental life. She wishes Karen would do the same. She might be much happier if she did live like Tessa.

Despite the tension between the women, they all have a nice time at the yacht party and are ready to head to the islands.

Sunday: Day 6-The Bahamas

Everyone goes to plan their next cruise and book a cruise for the Christmas Break in December. Karen finally books her family cruise. She knows her and William will have all of their family problems worked out by then. A family cruise will be a perfect place to rebuild. *Maybe I will be pregnant by then.*

Next, Peaches has planned an excursion for the women. "Okay ladies! Today we have an exciting day planned for you all. We are going to get off the ship and go swim with dolphins and we are going to end the afternoon with lunch prepared by a personal chef."

Throughout the day, Karen attempts to get close to Tessa, but every time Tessa turns her back or walks away. When they were swimming with the dolphins, Tessa swam to the other side of the tank to avoid contact with Karen.

Karen was so confused. *She must really be jealous of my life. Poor thing.*

Monday: Day 7-The Bahamas

As Tessa and Khrystina are sitting at a restaurant in the Bahamas, Tessa receives a message. "Oh my!" She says, clutching her imaginary pearls.

"What is it?" Khrystina asks.
Tessa holds up her phone to show Khrystina the image that is on her screen. It is a picture of William and Charlice kissing at Wolf Trap. Someone sent the picture to Tessa. "You know who that man is don't you?"
"No!" Khrystina responds but she knows who it is. That picture is similar to the photos that Peaches had shown her when they were about to board the ship. "Who is that?"

Tessa smiles, "This is the dear and loving husband of Mrs. Karen Lime. You know the man that she has been bragging about all cruise. The man that walks on water. The man that worships the ground that she walks on. The perfect FAITHFUL man. Her hubby."

"Oh My!" Khrystina says.

"Oh my is right" She walkin' 'round here like she is better than everybody. And look at this. He is running around with somebody else. I can't wait to burst her bougie bubble."

Khrystina interrupts. "Let's hold off on that for a while. Let her enjoy her trip. We are all in a foreign country. Plus, we don't know the whole story. Just don't say anything just yet. Okay?"

"You are right. I won't say anything for now. I just hope she doesn't set me off about something." Tessa takes a sip of her drink.

Khrystina texts Peaches, 'FYI: The pictures of William and Charlice are out around DC. You may have to tell Karen.'

Peaches text: Damn…Understood.

Tuesday: Day 8-Dominican Republic

Peaches and Khrystina explore the island together.
"How the hell did Tessa get those pictures?" Peaches asks.

Khrystina is taken aback by the tone in Peaches' voice. "I don't know. Someone texted them to her."

"Well it damn sure wasn't me. I will find out how she got them. If Karen sees those pictures or if someone tells her in some crazy way, she is going to lose it."

"Then you have to tell her Peaches." Khrystina interjects. "She is your friend. You would want someone, especially your friend to tell you. Wouldn't you?"

Peaches rolls her eyes because she hates when Khrystina is right, "Yes my friend. You are correct. I will take her aside and tell her."

Wednesday: Day 9-Dominican Republic

Peaches, Karen and some of the other women on the cruise take a tour of the DR.

Khrystina and Tessa decide to go shopping together. Tessa jokes that she hopes there are some TJ Maxx and Ross in the DR.

Khrystina and Tessa walk off.
A conversation ensues about the pictures.

"The picture is Karen's husband and that is his real estate agent or at least that is what he told Karen." Khrystina says.

"Oh okay!" Tessa thinks. "Well, I'm not going to say anything. It is not my place to share that information because I don't have the pictures. Plus, I don't want to be a part of that whole messy situation."

Khrystina agrees. "Oh absolutely! It is messy or at least it is going to be. Bless Karen's heart. She wants to be a good wife."

When they get back to the ship, Tessa calls Sandy and tells her all about the pictures of William and Charlice. "Sandy, you need to tell Lou so she can warn Charlice. This shit is about to hit the fan when the ship returns to Baltimore. Because once Karen finds out, no one in that shop is going to be safe."

Sandy laughs, "You are correct. I will pass the information off to Lou. We will all strap up. Bye girl! Have fun!"

***

Peaches and Karen take a tour bus to Saona Island for a walk in the white sands and a quick swim. Karen knows this is the perfect time to share her thoughts about Dr. Wells. She has Peaches all to herself with no audience.

But before Karen could mention it, Peaches asks, "How is the therapy going with you and the fam?"

"I am so glad you asked. It is going horribly wrong. Why did you refer to her to me?" Karen gets up close to Peaches' face. "Did you get some kind of kickback? Dr. Wells is doing waaaayyyy too much. I need her to focus on getting William back in the house. And I thought I told you THAT!"

Peaches takes a step back, and gives Karen a *Bitch, have you lost your mind AGAIN* look.

"First of all, Imma need you to back up. Back up from me and watch your mouth. You came to me. YOU asked for advice. YOU asked for a reference."

Karen tried to interject but Peaches was on a roll. "Shut the fuck up and let me finish." Peaches is screaming directly in Karen's face.

Peaches was trying to feel sorry for Karen but now she knows she is crazy. Peaches could care less now about her feelings and her family. "Make this the last time you talk to me like I am your subordinate. I'm not the one. I'm not like the rest of these people you look down on."

Karen takes a deep breath, "Is that a threat? Are you threatening me Peaches? Do I look like I am afraid of you?" Karen takes a step closer to Peaches. "You may tell everyone else what to do but not me. You promised me that you would get me the help that I needed for myself and my family. You set us up with a doctor who is trying to tear my family apart. Are you my friend? Or are you pretending to be my friend so you can sleep with my husband? Yeah, I knew you wanted my husband the first time we met. I saw how you were looking at him. You knew he had money and that's why you befriended me. You were trying to get close to me so you could get to him. Did you really think he would leave me for you? I knew your trick."

Everyone is staring at Karen and Peaches. All of the tourists, the tour guides and the locals are staring at Peaches and Karen and listening.

One of the tour guides walks over to Karen and Peaches and asks, "Hey ladies! Is everything okay? Do you ladies need any assistance?"

Karen and Peaches stare at each other in silence. They did not realize that they were surrounded by so many people on the beach. Peaches was hoping that no one recognized her. This was so embarrassing. It has been years since someone has made her go off the deep end.

Peaches now knows that Karen is losing her mind. Peaches grabs her beach bag and walks off.

I cannot and will not deal with her ever again… If I don't get my ass back to the ship, I am going to jail today. And this is the wrong place to go to jail. My friends and family will never see me again. I should have shown her the picture of her husband and that woman, and maybe she would have gone into the ocean and never returned. Crazy Ass Bitch.

Karen and Peaches ride back to the ship on the same tour bus and sit far apart. Staring into the distance in silence.

Thursday: Day 10-Puerto Rico

It's Lobster Night. Everyone who loves seafood was going to show up and have as many lobsters as they could eat.

All of the ladies from Peaches' entourage are sitting at the table together along with two random women from Delaware. They drove down from Delaware to board the ship.

Karen decides to come to dinner, but she stops at the Customer Service Desk in the main dinner room and asks if she could change her seat. She does not want to sit with the ladies tonight since she and Peaches are not in a good space. Karen feels like *Peaches owes me an apology for going off on me in front of so many people. She just might snap on me again in front of the rest of the ladies.*

The dining room supervisor looks for another seat but is unable to accommodate Karen's request. After all, it is Lobster Night so the dining room is packed.

Karen is disappointed but decides to sit with the women and just stay quiet.

She walks to the table and everyone is there. There are some unfamiliar women sitting there.

The ladies are having a conversation about marriages and infidelity. Should you stay with your husband if he is cheating? Should you stay and get yourself a side piece? Should you leave and take half of his money? What about the kids? What about your in-laws?

Karen sits and does not engage in the discussion. She is just listening and thinking about her marriage. She knows that William will never cheat on her so she doesn't need to be a part of the conversation.

Someone asks, "If your friend's husband is cheating, and you knew, would you tell her?"

Tessa speaks and says, "I would tell my friend. But I would only tell if there was proof to go with it." Tessa does not like drama, especially hear say.

Another woman says, "No, if you are a friend, you need to stay out of their business. If the woman really knows her husband, then the woman would know if her husband was cheating. All the signs would be there. Women are just too dumb and blind to pay attention to the signs. They only see what they want to see."

"What are the signs?" One of the ladies asks.

"One: Your Husband doesn't spend time with you; Two: Your husband doesn't have sex with you and Three: Your husband moves out of the house."

Miss Hattie says, "No1 I would not tell because it's not my business. A wife should know her husband and be able to tell if he is cheating if she paid attention to the signs. The man will always show you the signs. They are too dumb to keep clean. Women need to pay more attention. That's what's wrong with the younger generation. These women pay attention to everything else and everybody else. They never pay attention to their own lives and business. That's why the divorce rate is so high."

Miss Hattie looks at Karen and says, "That's why your husband left you. You paid him no attention and he found someone that would." Miss Hattie didn't know if Karen's husband was really cheating. She only knew what she overheard at the vision board party, what she heard on the ship and she saw the pictures. That was enough for her to make an assumption.

"Mind your own business Miss Hattie. You don't even know what you're talking about." Karen screams looking at the old woman.

"Yes, I do. There are pictures of him hugged up with his real estate agent. Everybody has seen them. You've been bragging about your wonderful husband and it turns out that he ain't shit. He is just like the rest of the men. A cheater."

Everyone is silent. Peaches, Tessa and Khrystina look at each other. Then look over at Karen. At that moment, they all felt sorry for her.

Karen finding out about the picture triggers something in her. She jumps up from the table and immediately starts yelling at random people.

She bumps into a server and knocks a plate out of his hands. She calls him Sergio. "Get away from me Sergio. You have done enough. It's your fault. You ruined my family."

The ladies at the table just watch. None of them are sure what to do. So they just watch as Karen walks away.

She continues to walk away. She is dazed and confused walking out of the dining room. "William, how could you do this to me? To our family. How could you embarrass me like this? I trusted you. Yelling at imaginary William. "Daddy, I need you. William cheated on me with that woman. What am I supposed to do now? Daddy please help me." Karen starts to cry as she reaches out for her dad.

She stops a young couple headed into the dining room. "Now Willow and Will J. He is still your dad. He still loves you even though he has chosen to abandon us."

The young couple smile and continue on into the dining room. Empathetic to Karen's behavior. They conclude that she must have had too much to drink.

Karen sort of gets her thoughts together. She has to get out of here.

So she runs back to her room and gets some cash. She knows she doesn't have to take her ID because she has her sea pass and cash. She leaves the room and spends the night on the top deck of the ship.

Friday: Day 11- Puerto Rico

Early that morning, Karen gets off the ship. She must be back on the ship by 4 pm. She decides she is going to stay off the ship the entire day. *I don't want to talk to any of those women. None of them are my friends, including Peaches. I cannot believe Peaches would betray me like that.* She is so upset with Peaches.

Karen visits local restaurants and shops. At one of the shops, she meets a nice woman named Patsy and they strike up a conversation.

"They have some nice things in these shops." Karen says.

"If you like these things, you might like to see some of the items at some of the local shops. I can drive you to some of

278

them, if you would like." Patsy offers. "The items near the ship are always overpriced."

"Why sure! That would be nice." Karen goes off with Patsy to visit some of the local shops for cheaper items.

Saturday: Day 12-At Sea

No Karen in sight.

No one is worried about Karen. Everyone thinks she is wandering around the ship or in her room trying to avoid everyone because she is embarrassed.

Peaches suggest, "She just wants someone to chase after her. Let her alone. She will come out when she is finished pouting."

Sunday: Day 13-At Sea

Still no Karen. No one has seen her.

Now the ladies are worried.

They meet for lunch to decide who is going to knock on her door.

Peaches decides, "I will go to Guest Services and do a wellness check."

When Peaches goes to Guest Services, the representative tells Peaches that Karen, based on her sea pass activity was in the casino this morning and used her sea pass to get a few drinks.

"Thank you!" Peaches says. *I knew that bitch was playing games with us. Got us all worried for nothing. So I'm glad to know that she is okay! She just really wants to be left alone. I respect that. I will let her have that.*

Monday: Day 14-Arrive back in Baltimore at 7am

That Monday morning Peaches has arranged to meet all the ladies at an early breakfast. They all had departure times for10:00 am. The ship had docked in Baltimore at around 7:30 am.

Khrystina is a little upset with Peaches. She knows her friend. They met at Temple University and have been friends ever since. Khrystina knows that Peaches could be a little messy but Peaches had many good qualities that made her a great friend.

Before everyone arrives in the dining room, Khrystina decides that she has to talk to Peaches about the incidents at the dinner the night before.

"Peaches, I must admit. I feel some kind of way that you would hold that information from Karen. If it was my husband with another woman would you tell me that he was seen with another woman out in public?"

Peaches holds Khrystina's hands, "Of course, I would tell you Krissy. Karen's situation is different." Peaches tries to explain to Khrystina, "I wanted to tell her but I wanted Karen to enjoy the trip. She needed the getaway. I didn't want her to know until we got back home. I even considered telling her on the very last day just before the ship docked. I probably would have gone to go talk to her

280

last night, if Tessa hadn't gotten into that altercation with those Delaware women. That damn Hattie had to open up her mouth."

The conversation last night led into a debate at the dinner table. Then the conversation turned into an argument between Tessa and the women from Delaware. The argument turned into a fist fight in the main dinner hall. Lobsters and seafood were flying everywhere as Tessa and one of the Delaware ladies tussled around on the floor and under the table. Peaches and the rest of the ladies tried to break it up but it took security, the servers and some of the crew to break up the brawl. Peaches spent the rest of her evening trying to make sure Tessa stayed calm and did not get locked up somewhere. After all Tessa works for the federal government and could not afford to lose that good government job.

Karen had missed the fight and had no idea that there was a fight about her husband William cheating. By then, she had left the dining hall because of Miss Hattie's comment.

"Have you seen Karen?" Khrystina asks.

"Nope! I guess she is still upset with me. I guess she doesn't want to see us."

The remaining women join Peaches and Khrystina. They have a wonderful breakfast discussing the ups and downs of their trip. They are all ready to get back home and jump back into their regularly scheduled lives. Around 10:15, all of the women head off the ship.

As they head off the ship, Peaches asks Tessa, "Were you and Karen together? Have you seen Karen?"

Tessa laughs, "I haven't seen her in days. I stopped hanging out with her when she started belittling me about shopping at TJ Maxx and Ross."

Peaches asked, "Did you not find it kinda strange that you had not seen her, since you two had been hanging out so much?"
"Someone needs to go knock on Karen's door. She is mad at me so I know she won't answer. Who will volunteer to go?"

No one wants to do it since the outburst Karen had. Everyone was afraid.

"Never mind." Peaches says, "She probably left already." So Peaches and the ladies got off the ship and headed to their vehicles.

When Peaches was headed to her car, that is when she spotted William.

He sees her too, so he walks towards her smiling. "Hey Peaches! Did you and Karen have a nice trip?"

"Hey William! What are you doing here?" Peaches was shocked he was there and a little angry thinking about the pictures of him and Charlice all hugged up.

"I am waiting here for Karen. Before she left, she told me that she needed a ride home. Is she still on the ship? Leave it to her to forget something and have to go back to get it."

Hesitating, Peaches stutters, "I am not sure. I thought Karen had already gotten off the ship."
"Nope! I showed up early so I have been here for about an hour or so. I have not seen her. She must have gone back to get something. Did she say anything this morning about getting off later? I have not seen her nor has she called me."

Both Peaches and William tried calling Karen, but the phone went to voicemail.

They head back to the terminal to talk with someone. They approach an agent and explain that they are unable to locate someone that was traveling with them. They give the agent Karen's information.

The agent looks up the departure log. "According to our records, Mrs. Lime re-boarded the ship in Puerto Rico. It also showed that she departed the ship this morning at 8 am."

"I don't understand." William says, confused. "Karen knew I was picking her up. She would have called me if her plans changed."

Peaches knew Karen was mad with her and didn't suspect anything from her leaving the ship early. Karen looked embarrassed the last time she saw her at the dinner table in the main dining hall. *Where can she be?*

Peaches wondered if she should tell William why Karen was upset. Should she tell him that someone sent a picture of him and a woman named Charlice? Peaches is really worried about Karen. Peaches decides not to tell William about the pictures. If he is known in the city, then I am probably sure that somebody has told him. He could not be living under a rock with a wife like Karen, who always wants to be seen.

Peaches has never met Charlice. She only heard of her. They didn't run in the same circles. Peaches was curious now. All this time, she thought Karen was reading into the realtor way too much. Now she was wrong. If Peaches had believed Karen, she could have done some digging around the city about the girl. *Where the hell is Karen? She just vanished.*

William thinks about all the signs of distress that Karen has shown him. The suicide note that the kids found last week. The pill bottle on the counter, the constant outburst. *What have I done?*

William, with tears in his eyes, looks at Peaches, "Where is Karen? What the hell did you do with my wife, Peaches?"

"She wasn't ready for this kind of distraction he caused her. It was bad enough she found him attractive, but having an attractive man in her home was just asking for trouble."
— *J. C. Valentine, <u>Stranded</u>*

REFERENCES

All quotes were cited from goodreads.com
https://www.goodreads.com/quotes

For book signings, and speaking engagements, please
contact T.C. McFarland at:
allchallengesmastered@gmail.com